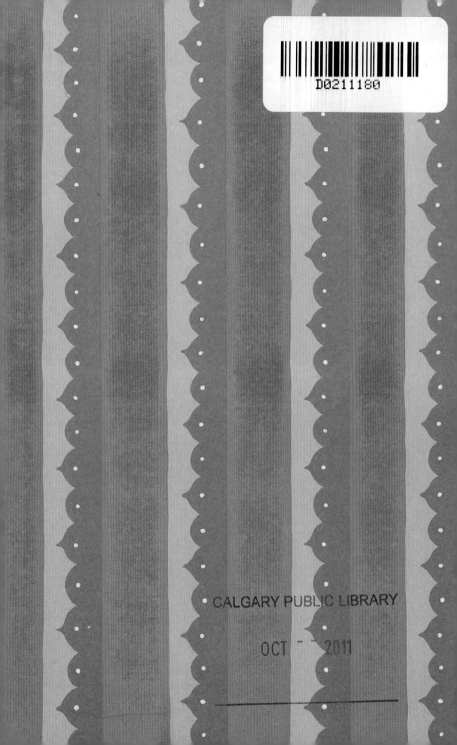

A LAURA MARLIN MYSTERY

KIDNAP IN THE CARIBBEAN

Also by Lauren St John

Laura Marlin Mysteries

Dead Man's Cove

The White Giraffe Quartet

The White Giraffe
Dolphin Song
The Last Leopard
The Elephant's Tale

A LAURA MARLIN MYSTERY

KIDNAP IN THE CARIBBEAN

Lauren St John

Illustrated by David Dean

Orion
Children's Books

First published in Great Britain in 2011
by Orion Children's Books
a division of the Orion Publishing Group Ltd
Orion House
5 Upper St Martin's Lane
London WC2H 9EA
An Hachette UK Company

3 5 7 9 10 8 6 4 2

The Orion Publishing Group's policy is to use papers that are
natural, renewable and recyclable products and made from wood
grown in sustainable forests. The logging and manufacturing
processes are expected to conform to the environmental
regulations of the country of origin.

A catalogue record for this book is available
from the British Library

Printed in Great Britain by Clays Ltd, St Ives plc

ISBN 978 1 4440 0021 4

www.laurenstjohn.com

www.orionbooks.com

For Virginia McKenna,
my wildlife hero, who, like me,
believes that sea creatures need love too. . .

'IMAGINE WINNING A CARIBBEAN CRUISE TO AN ISLAND WITH *THREE HUNDRED AND SIXTY-FIVE* BEACHES – ONE FOR EVERY DAY OF THE YEAR. LADIES AND GENTLEMEN, BOYS AND GIRLS, THE SAND IS SO WHITE IT SPARKLES. PICTURE YOURSELF IN PARADISE. IMAGINE LYING IN A HAMMOCK SIPPING COCONUT MILK WHILE DOLPHINS FROLIC IN A TURQUOISE LAGOON, SO CLOSE YOU CAN ALMOST REACH OUT AND TOUCH THEM.'

It was a grey, rainy Saturday in St Ives and, as much as she adored her new home, Laura Marlin could think

I

of nothing better than doing exactly that. She especially liked the dolphin part. By the look of things she was not alone. Despite the drizzle, a crowd was gathering around the speaker – a woman in a sky-blue shirt with the words Fantasy Travel on the pocket. An old-fashioned pillbox hat in a matching blue was perched on top of her sleek reddish-brown bob. She was sheltering beneath a beach umbrella patterned with smiling suns, holding a basket filled with mauve bits of paper.

'AND THAT'S NOT ALL. ONCE YOU GET TO THE BEAUTIFUL ISLAND OF ANTIGUA, WE'LL THROW IN A FREE WEEK AT A FIVE STAR HOTEL FOR YOU AND A FRIEND, PLUS RETURN FLIGHTS. IF YOU WANT TO COME BACK TO THE RAIN, THAT IS, HA HA!'

Skye's wet nose nudged Laura and she gave his furry ears a rub. She knew she should be getting home because her uncle was taking her for a fish and chip lunch at the Porthminster Beach Café, but she was intrigued to hear what one had to do to win a trip to paradise. Rain or shine, Laura loved St Ives more than anywhere else on earth, but that didn't mean she didn't long to travel, particularly if it involved basking in the sun in hammocks, or paddling with dolphins in turquoise lagoons.

Until a few months ago when Laura had discovered she had an uncle she never knew existed and moved to number 28 Ocean View Terrace in St Ives, Cornwall, a seaside resort on the southern tip of England, she'd spent her whole life at Sylvan Meadows Children's Home in a northern town prone to Arctic temperatures. There, her room had overlooked a car park and a concrete playground – a vista so dull she'd preferred to lose herself in stories.

Over the years, books had become her window on the world. Her favourites were those about her hero, Detective Inspector Matt Walker, a genius at outwitting deadly criminals. Laura had spent hours staring out of the window wishing she could have a life of excitement like the characters in her books, but at Sylvan Meadows nothing ever happened. There were no sinister characters or mysterious lights in the night.

That had changed from almost the moment she arrived in St Ives. Before she knew it she was up to her ears in enough adventures to keep most people happy for a lifetime. Laura, however, was no ordinary girl. Far from quenching her thirst for excitement, she had become all the more determined to make a career out of it.

Her fervent hope was that when she was older and an ace detective like Matt, her travels would take her to places like the canals of Venice, the vampire-haunted mountains of Transylvania, or the African savannah, where lions roamed. In the meantime, she couldn't think of anything more wonderful than winning a trip to a palm-fringed island in the Caribbean.

The only downside of such a life would be leaving Skye and Tariq who, next to her uncle, was her favourite person in the world.

'DOES THIS SOUND LIKE THE HOLIDAY OF YOUR DREAMS?' demanded the Fantasy Travel representative.

'Are you kidding?' cried a harassed-looking mum,

practically mowing Laura down with an oversized buggy that looked as if it had been designed to climb Everest. 'I'll take ten tickets so I have ten times the luck.'

Laura rolled her eyes and moved with Skye to a new spot. Several people shrank away from the Siberian husky who, with his hypnotic blue eyes and thick, grey-darkening-to-black coat, resembled a wolf. Laura grinned to herself until she noticed a young couple gesturing at the jagged silver line in Skye's fur where his right foreleg should have been. They were whispering behind their hands. Laura bent down and hugged the husky protectively. Skye might only have three limbs (he'd lost one after being hit by a car as a puppy), but he was worth a hundred of most dogs with four.

'And you're worth a thousand of people like them,' she told him in a whisper loud enough for them to hear. She was about to kiss him on the muzzle when he gave a sudden snarl.

Laura glanced up and saw, with a slight shock, that the Fantasy Travel woman was gazing directly at her.

'We haven't got all day. How much are the tickets?' called out a man in a green sweatshirt with a frog on the front.

The woman switched her attention to the frog man. Her voice boomed down Fore Street. 'ONE POUND. FOR THE TRIFLING SUM OF ONE POUND, YOU AND A FRIEND COULD BE SAILING AWAY ON A LUXURY CRUISE.'

There was a stampede to buy raffle tickets. The drizzle had stopped but the buildings were still dripping, and

Laura watched the frenzy from the shelter of the bakery awning. It was late March. Spring had sprung, but so far it had, the weathermen admitted, been a washout. Record amounts of rain had meant that Laura and Calvin Redfern had spent many sodden days walking Skye and Lottie, her uncle's wolfhound. It was a challenge attempting to towel them dry afterwards. Rowenna, their new housekeeper, was forever burning sandalwood incense in the hallway in a bid to eliminate the smell of wet dog.

'House smells like a monastery these days,' her uncle would grumble every time he came home, but he'd wink at Laura as he said it. It was obvious he regarded Rowenna – a big-boned country girl who'd replaced Mrs Webb, their previous housekeeper – as the best thing since clotted cream scones. So did Laura. Rowenna was sunny-tempered, loved dogs and had a fine line in rhubarb crumble and custard, whereas Mrs Webb had always reminded Laura of a tarantula.

Laura watched the crowd around the beach umbrella disperse, some people clutching handfuls of mauve raffle tickets.

'Three days till the draw,' the harassed-looking mother told her friend. 'Don't think I'll sleep, I'll be so excited.' She glanced down at the buggy, in which a red-faced infant was building up to a crescendo of screaming. 'Not that sleep's an option.'

Laura noticed the Fantasy Travel representative staring at her again.

'Fine animal,' the woman said, nodding in Skye's direction. 'Siberian husky, is he? Used to have one myself.

5

Very regal they are. Think they're royalty, I suspect.'

Laura was so thrilled to have met a fellow Siberian husky owner that she was across the cobbled street before she could stop herself, her usual wariness of strangers evaporating in an instant.

'Did you, really? Aren't they amazing? Skye's the best dog on earth. He's my best friend. Actually, I have two best friends. Skye and Tariq. He's from Bangladesh.'

'Lucky you. Most people count themselves fortunate to have one friend.' Up close, the woman was wearing rather too much makeup and had a diamond in her front tooth. Laura thought that Fantasy Travel must be a very successful company if its agents could afford precious gems in their teeth. The woman bent to pet Skye, but he bared his sharp fangs.

'Skye!' Laura said reprovingly.

The woman chuckled. 'Like I said, they think they're royalty.' She took a ticket from her basket. 'How would you like to win a trip to paradise, my dear?'

Laura hesitated. 'I only have two pounds and I was planning to buy some coconut ice. It's this pink and white fudge with coconut bits. What was your husky's name?'

'Coconut ice? Why would you need a lump of pink sugar when you can eat real coconut until it's coming out your ears in Antigua?'

'That's only if I win,' Laura pointed out, 'and the chances of that happening are slim to non-existent. I've never won a thing in my life.'

The Fantasy Travel woman smiled and the diamond winked. 'You never know. Miracles do happen.'

It was true. Miracles did happen. How else could Laura have been plucked from the dreary confines of Sylvan Meadows orphanage after eleven long years and deposited in a room with a sea view in the home of her uncle, where she was quite blissfully happy. Especially since Skye was allowed to sleep on her bed every night.

It was the possibility of being able to repay Calvin Redfern for his kindness that won her over. Money was tight and there was no way her uncle could afford a holiday otherwise. Laura held out a pound coin. 'All right, I'll buy one ticket.'

'Just the one? I suppose if it's a lucky ticket, one is all it takes.'

Laura studied the ticket. It was about three times the size of a postage stamp and had the number 252 printed on it. She closed her eyes and made a wish.

When she opened her eyes, the woman was watching her intently.

Disconcerted, Laura said: 'What was the dog's name?'

'What dog?'

'Your husky.'

'Oh, of course. It was . . . ' She cleared her throat. 'Hudson. His name was Hudson.'

Sensing that the woman had lost interest in the subject of Siberian huskies and was probably keen to attract more customers, Laura put the ticket safely in her purse and set off down Fore Street.

A voice rang out behind her. 'LADIES AND GENTLEMEN, CAN I INTEREST YOU IN A DREAM VOYAGE TO A TROPICAL ISLAND?'

7

As she and Skye neared the alley that was a shortcut – via a set of steep stone steps – to Ocean View Terrace, Laura glanced over her shoulder. The Fantasy Travel representative, her beach umbrella and her tickets to paradise were all gone!

It seemed so impossible that the woman could have vanished in under two minutes that Laura walked back a little way, convinced the rain was blurring her vision.

For a moment, she wondered if the whole thing had been a product of her over-active imagination. But the ticket was still in her purse, now speckled purple with drizzle.

She was halfway home when she remembered that Hudson – or, at least, TM Hudson & Sons – was the name of the bakery opposite where the Fantasy Travel rep had been standing. More than likely it was a coincidence that she happened to have had a husky of the same name. After all, what possible motive could she have had for inventing one? But then Matt Walker always said that there was no such thing as a coincidence.

~ 2 ~

'**A WATCHED POT** never boils,' declared Mrs Crabtree.

Laura and Skye were sitting on the stone wall outside number 28 Ocean View Terrace. They were waiting for the postman and gazing down the hill at Porthmeor Beach, where grey waves steamed up to the shore beneath a sullen sky. Between the house and the beach was a cemetery. On sunny days it was serene and quite lovely, but on stormy days like this the Celtic crosses, twisted tree and jackdaws pecking among the crumbling gravestones made it feel eerie.

Laura glanced at the sky. It was threatening to rain again. The Fantasy Travel woman had told her that the

9

raffle draw was taking place on Monday and that she'd be notified soon afterwards if she'd won, but today was Thursday and so far she'd heard nothing. Laura would not have admitted it to Mrs Crabtree, but she was losing hope that she'd be going off on a luxury cruise any time soon.

'I'm not watching for a pot; I'm waiting for a letter telling me I've won a trip to paradise,' Laura told her neighbour.

Mrs Crabtree stabbed a weed with her trowel. Though retired, she liked to dress for effect, and today she was in yellow gardening gloves and a leopard print coat. 'There's a reason people often use "trouble" and "paradise" in the same sentence, you know. The two words tend to go together.'

'Why's that?' asked Laura, but Mrs Crabtree's response was drowned out by furious barking from Skye.

The postman scowled as he handed Laura a bill for her uncle, taking care to stay out of range of the husky's jaws. 'I'll be demanding danger money if this goes on much longer, I will,' he complained. 'Day after day, you and that werewolf lying in wait. It's not good for my heart.'

Laura's own heart sank as it became obvious that there was no post for her. 'He's not a werewolf or even a wolf,' she said, clinging to Skye's collar. 'He's a Siberian husky. And he's normally very sweet-natured.' She didn't add that, although he was mostly very gentle, he had strong objections to strangers approaching Laura.

She eyed the postman's bulging sack. 'Are you sure you haven't got anything for me? Maybe the letter's slipped down the back of your mailbag, or been delivered to the wrong address. Oh, please can you check again?'

The postman took no notice of her. He handed Mrs Crabtree a package and stamped off down the street muttering something about 'kids today'.

'What makes you so sure you've won?' Mrs Crabtree opened her parcel and gazed approvingly at a carton of rose feed. 'It could be a scam, like so many of these things. I mean, have you ever met anyone who's won so much as a packet of shortbread in a raffle, let alone a holiday or millions of pounds? I never have and I've been around for six and a half decades. I think it's a con.'

'It's not a con,' Laura said stubbornly. 'Lots of people bought tickets. Besides, the travel rep who was selling them used to have a Siberian husky, and huskies are very choosy about who they spend their time with so she must be all right. Anyhow, I had a dream that I'd won the competition.'

She didn't tell Mrs Crabtree that the dream had been more of a nightmare. In it, the Fantasy Travel woman had kidnapped her on a pirate ship and taken her, not to Antigua, but to a plank suspended over a shaft that led to the earth's core. As molten fires seethed below her, some unseen assassin had tried to push Laura in. She'd been very relieved to wake up in her own bed with Skye licking her face.

'Stay away from raffles and lotteries,' Mrs Crabtree counselled her. 'Hard work, that's what earns holidays or makes fortunes. Sweat and elbow grease.'

Laura didn't respond. Her uncle had told her much the same thing. He'd said that the chances of Laura winning them a free trip to the Caribbean were thousands, if not millions, to one, and that in the unlikely event she did scoop first prize, there was bound to be a catch. They'd discover they had to row themselves to Antigua on a raft, or there'd be loads of hidden expenses on the trip and they'd be bankrupted.

Mrs Crabtree's comment about hard work reminded Laura that she still had a ton of homework to do. Even though the term was about to end, Mr Gillbert was merciless when it came to piling it on.

Skye did his '*Pleeease*-won't-you-take-me-for-a-walk?' whine. Laura ran her hand over his thick coat. 'Not today,' she told him, looking wistfully down at Porthmeor Beach. 'I have to finish my geography project. In two more days, it'll be school holidays and you'll get tons of walks because —'

She got no further because Mrs Crabtree suddenly gasped, cast aside the box of rose feed, and checked her blonde curls for neatness.

A gleaming stretch limousine with blacked out windows was gliding up the street towards them.

'A movie star!' cried Mrs Crabtree. 'Must be. Of course, St Ives has always attracted artists, writers and other flamboyant folk. Ooh, I wonder who it is. Laura, let's try to get a good look if the chauffeur slows.'

Laura gripped Skye's collar and watched the limousine approach. The dark windscreen gave the impression that the car was driverless, directed by an invisible force.

To her surprise, the car sighed to a stop right in front of her. A chauffeur in a sharp suit and white shirt hopped out and, with a double take at Mrs Crabtree's leopard-print coat, started up the steps of number 28.

Laura experienced a moment of pure panic. The last time she'd seen a black car with dark windows, two members of the Straight A gang – the most evil and sophisticated crime syndicate in the world –had been inside it. She'd been ignorant of that at the time and the consequences had been catastrophic.

'Oh, my goodness, Laura, someone famous has come to visit your uncle!' cried Mrs Crabtree as the chauffeur rang the doorbell. 'Perhaps a Government Minister? Why are you standing there like a dummy? Quick, run and see who he's after.'

But Laura couldn't move. She was mute, rooted to the spot.

Mrs Crabtree gave her a sharp poke. When that didn't work, she called out: 'Young man, if you're looking for Calvin Redfern, he's not in right now. Can I help you? Will you be quiet, Skye! Any more of that and my hearing aid will explode.'

The chauffeur descended the steps three at a time. 'Thank you, ma'am, but I'm not here to see a gentleman. I have urgent business with the lady of the house – a Miss Marlin. Are you familiar with her?'

Another awful thought occurred to Laura. What if the chauffeur was not a member of the Straight A gang but really was a Government Minister come to lure Calvin Redfern away on some special assignment that would result in Laura being sent back to Sylvan Meadows? Or what if someone with a red pen and too much power at Social Services had read about her adventures at Dead Man's Cove and sent a lawyer to inform Calvin Redfern that he was a thoroughly unsuitable guardian and that she'd be better off back in the orphanage?

She tried to catch Mrs Crabtree's eye, but it was too late. Her neighbour piped up, 'This is Laura right here. And who, might I ask, are you?'

A smile lit the face of the chauffeur, a black man who could easily have been a movie star himself. '*You're* Laura Marlin. And there I was picturing someone much . . . older. Not, I'm certain, that it makes any difference. Miss Marlin, would you come this way, please? I have something for you.'

Laura backed away in alarm, keeping Skye close to her.

The chauffeur raised his eyebrows. 'I must say, that's not quite the reaction I was expecting.' He smiled again. 'No matter. You're right to be wary of strangers.'

He returned to the limousine and produced a dozen pink balloons and a large, thick pink envelope, all of which he placed in Laura's reluctant hands.

'You didn't tell me it was your birthday, Laura,' exclaimed Mrs Crabtee.

'It's not.' Laura was braced for a trick or a trap. She and Calvin Redfern, a former detective who had a top-secret job investigating illegal fishing in the waters around Cornwall, had recently been responsible for the arrests of several key members of the Straight A's, and the gang was notoriously vengeful.

She needn't have worried. The chauffeur merely touched the brim of his hat and gave another grin. 'Goodbye and good luck, Miss Marlin.' He nodded at Mrs Crabtree as he climbed into the limousine. 'Goodbye, ma'am. If you don't mind me saying so, that's some outfit you have on. Quite striking. Brightens up a cloudy day, it does.'

Laura started forward. 'Wait,' she cried. 'What company are you from? Who sent you?'

But the chauffeur's dark window was already sliding shut and he didn't appear to hear her. Jackdaws rose screeching from the cemetery as the limousine purred away.

'Aren't you going to open your letter?' demanded Mrs Crabtree, still glowing from the chauffeur's compliment.

Laura turned the envelope over. Her name was typed on the front but there was no other mark on it.

Mrs Crabtree said impatiently: 'Here, give it to me.' She ripped the envelope open without ceremony, withdrew a pink card and read aloud:

'*Dear Laura Marlin,*

'*Congratulations from all at Fantasy Holidays Ltd on winning a luxury cruise for two to the beautiful Caribbean island of—*'

She had to pause then because Laura squealed with delight and started leaping around like a crazy person. Skye threw his head back and howled with excitement.

'*—Antigua. The enclosed voucher* – shush, Skye, you're giving me a headache – *includes a voyage from Falmouth, Cornwall to Antigua on the Ocean Empress, a week's all-inclusive accommodation at the five-star Blue Haven resort, a helicopter tour of Montserrat's volcano, and return flights to the United Kingdom.*'

Mrs Crabtree engulfed Laura in her furry leopard coat. 'My dear girl, I take everything back. Your holiday competition is genuine after all. Forgive me for being such an old cynic. Oh, I could not possibly be happier for you and Calvin. Two people more deserving of a holiday I simply can't imagine.'

When at last Laura managed to extricate herself from Mrs Crabtree's embrace, she walked up the steps of 28 Ocean View Terrace in a joyful daze. It was impossible to take in. The winning mauve ticket had *her* name on it. She and her uncle were going on the trip of a lifetime to the Caribbean. She'd be able to pay him back for his kindness. They'd be sipping coconut milk in hammocks and swimming with dolphins in turquoise lagoons.

It was only as the door creaked shut behind her that Mrs Crabtree's warning came back to her: 'There's a reason people often put "trouble" and "paradise" in the same sentence, you know. The two words tend to go together.'

3

'**WE'RE NOT GOING** and that's final,' said Calvin Redfern.

Laura stared at her uncle in dismay. The moment he'd walked in the door, she'd pounced on him and told him the good news. His face was lined with exhaustion, but she'd fully expected him to whirl her off her feet and do a dance of happiness at the prospect of a free holiday. Instead he'd reacted as if she'd set her mattress on fire.

'But why? I don't understand.'

He ticked off his objections on his fingers. a) It was too sudden. What kind of travel firm expected them to pack their bags and depart on an ocean voyage with only two day's notice? b) Who would look after Skye?

'Tariq!' Laura said triumphantly. 'I've already checked with him and he said he can't think of anything nicer than looking after his favourite husky for a couple of weeks. You know his foster dad is a vet so Skye will be in very good hands.'

Her uncle continued as if she hadn't spoken.

'And c) I couldn't possibly take leave from work. This is our busiest time of the year. We're worried about the rise in illegal bluefin tuna imports.'

Laura said nothing. She had only been in Cornwall for a little over three months but it seemed to her that every week was the busiest of the year in her uncle's job. She'd never known anyone who worked so hard.

'Anyway, as I've said before, there's bound to be a catch,' he continued. 'The *Ocean Empress* will turn out to be a rubber dinghy with a leak. If you check the small print you can be sure you'll find dozens of hidden charges on the trip.'

He refused to relent even when Laura produced vouchers and documents guaranteeing payment for all meals, accommodation, flights for the whole two weeks of their journey, plus a travellers' cheque with $200 spending money on it – a gift from the competition organisers.

'It's not as simple as that,' said Calvin Redfern.

'Why?' demanded Laura.

'Laura, try to understand that I'd love to go as much as you would. It's just that we're having a crisis at work at the moment and I can't be spared.'

There was a tense moment as they faced each other across the kitchen table. Surely the bluefin tuna could manage without him for a week or two, Laura thought, and then immediately felt guilty for being so selfish.

She had a flashback to the stormy winter's night she'd arrived in St Ives. She'd never forgotten her first impression of her uncle. He'd been silhouetted in the doorway of 28 Ocean View Terrace with his wolfhound at his side, exuding a barely controlled strength. She'd been terrified. However, she'd quickly come to realise that he was the kindest man on earth. Now she loved him like a father – her real father, said to be an American, having vanished without trace after a brief romance with the mother she'd never known.

But as nice as he was, Calvin Redfern was a grown up and grown ups quite often put practical considerations ahead of fun. They liked to say things such as, 'Life is for living. It's not a dress rehearsal.' But that only applied if they weren't thinking about their taxes or the mess in your room. Or the many reasons why they couldn't go on a dream holiday to the Caribbean.

The telephone trilled, making them both jump. Calvin Redfern picked it up. The conversation was brief and Laura knew what her uncle was going to tell her even before he hung up.

'As you've probably gathered, that was Tariq's foster father. A relative is gravely ill and he and his wife have to leave for Delhi on the first available flight. They're not sure when they'll be back and they've asked whether it would be possible for Tariq to stay with us for the holidays. Naturally, I said yes.'

He opened the oven and took out a dish of macaroni

cheese. 'We can think of some fun things to do around Cornwall,' he said, ladling a steaming portion onto a plate for her. 'Maybe we could have a day out at the Eden Project.'

'Does that mean we're not going to be sailing away to the Caribbean after all?' Laura was so crushed she could hardly breathe.

'No, Laura, we're not going to be sailing away to Antigua.' Her uncle put an arm around her. His eyes were sad. It hurt him to hurt her. 'I'm sorry. I know how disappointed you are and it makes me feel ill to let you down. Unfortunately, duty calls. But I give you my word I'll make it up to you.'

Laura could tell that he'd made up his mind and it was no use arguing. She dug her fork into her macaroni. 'It's fine, Uncle Calvin. Really it is. It'll be wonderful to spend time with Tariq, and I'll get over it.'

But she knew she never would.

That night, Laura couldn't sleep at all. She tossed and turned for hours. At 2.10am, she wept on Skye's shoulder. Ordinarily, she would have been over the moon about having Tariq to stay for a couple of weeks. It's just that dream holidays don't come along every day, and she was devastated that her uncle had turned it down. She'd thought of suggesting that maybe she and Tariq could go instead, but guessed that wouldn't go down very well. Besides, who'd take care of Skye?

She was still awake at 2.48am when she heard the faint bleep of an incoming text on her uncle's mobile. Skye heard it too. Ears pricked, he jumped off the bed. A minute later, Laura heard the click of the front door. She flung off her duvet and peered through a slit in the blind.

When she'd first arrived at 28 Ocean View Terrace, the house had been full of secrets and her uncle had been a mysterious figure, haunted by his past and prone to taking midnight walks. Now they shared everything. Or did they? Where was Calvin Redfern going on such a wild, rainy night?

But he didn't go far. Coat collar turned up against the gale, he crossed the road to the graveyard, opened the gate and was immediately swallowed by the black shadows of the twisted pine. Nothing happened for a long time. It was too dark to make out what, if anything, he was up to, and Laura was about to return to her warm bed when she spotted an orange glow. Her uncle didn't smoke, which could only mean one thing. He had company. But who could he be meeting at 3am in the cemetery of all places?

Before she could ponder the matter further, her uncle swept through the cemetery gate, checked to see that he wasn't being observed, and hurried back into the house. Laura stayed at the window for a few minutes longer but no one else appeared. Somewhere in the night she heard a car engine rumble.

At length she fell into a disturbed sleep, waking bleary-eyed when her alarm went off at seven. Her uncle, usually long gone by the time Laura came down for breakfast, was in the kitchen making coffee. He seemed oddly cheerful.

'Good morning, Laura, I'm so pleased I caught you.' He handed her a mug and popped a slice of bread into the toaster for her. 'If you don't mind, I'd like to meet you when you finish school today. We have a lot to do and not much time to do it.'

Laura's eyes were open but her brain was still asleep. She tipped cornflakes into a bowl and stared at him blankly. 'I'm sorry, what is it we're supposed to be doing?'

He grinned. 'Laura, you have a very short memory. Surely you can't have forgotten that you've won us a trip and we're going to the Caribbean?'

It took a couple of seconds for the words to sink in, but even then Laura didn't get excited. She didn't trust what she was hearing. 'What's changed?' she asked warily.'I thought we couldn't go because you have a crisis at work, and the travel company didn't give us enough notice, and the *Ocean Empress* might be a leaky raft.'

Calvin Redfern held up his hand. 'I know what I said last night, Laura, but I was being unduly pessimistic. Exhaustion does that to me. It clouds my judgement. I called my boss first thing this morning and he has no problem with me taking leave under the circumstances. I also did some Internet research. The *Ocean Empress* looks quite impressive. In addition, I've checked with Tariq's foster parents and they're more than happy for him to stay with Skye and Rowenna, especially since you'd already mentioned that as a possibility. Don't worry about any of the details now. The main thing is, you're going on your dream holiday.'

Laura's head was whirling. The previous night her

uncle had been dead set against going to the Caribbean. This morning, just hours after his secret mission in the cemetery, there was this sudden change of heart. What was going on?

She shook herself. She was being paranoid. Winning the competition was a random, one-in-a-hundred-thousand thing. Whereas her uncle's meeting was probably something to do with bluefin tuna smugglers. What did it matter why the impossible had become possible in the space of a few hours? She'd got her wish. Within days, she'd be swimming with dolphins and sipping coconut milk in hammocks beneath pearly blue skies.

Then why did she suddenly feel so uneasy?

4

THE SHIP LOOKED like a floating wedding cake. That was what went through Laura's mind when she first caught a glimpse of it on their approach to Falmouth harbour. But nothing prepared her for the sheer magnificence of the vessel up close. The *Ocean Empress* was so tall that Laura got a crick in her neck staring up at her. She was a skyscraper of a boat, white as a swan with a single orange band lining her sleek side. Watery patterns of light danced around her prow.

'What I don't understand,' said Tariq in awe, 'is how something that big stays afloat. But,' he added hastily, 'it definitely will.'

Laura barely took in what he was saying. She was a bundle of nerves. In little more than an hour the *Ocean Empress* would set sail for the Caribbean and Laura was determined to ensure that nothing should happen to prevent her and Calvin Redfern from being on board when that happened.

Her fretting was justified. It had been a fraught forty-eight hours since her uncle had changed his mind and agreed to go to the Caribbean after all. There had been packing to organise, swimsuits to buy, arrangements to be made with Tariq's foster parents, and mountains of work for Calvin Redfern to get through in order to justify taking two weeks away from his job.

Laura was particularly jumpy because already that morning a whole series of things had gone wrong. She and her uncle had woken to discover the boiler was broken and there was no hot water – not good news when it was already so unseasonably cold that Rowenna had begun the day by chipping ice off the birdbath in the garden. Calvin Redfern's old car had delayed them further by refusing to start until he climbed out and pushed it, and a misunderstanding over where Tariq's foster parents would be dropping him off in Falmouth had made them later still.

To make matters worse, a cruel parking inspector had refused to allow Rowenna to wait even a minute close to the harbour, which meant that Tariq and his backpack were on the jetty with Laura and Skye while Rowenna had been left with no choice but to park the car on the other side of town.

Calvin Redfern was at the information booth on the jetty. Frowning slightly, he came over to them. When he saw no sign of Rowenna he looked more concerned still. 'Let's hope she gets back soon. Our ship sets sail within the hour and we can't possibly leave Tariq here on his own.'

He studied the folder of travel documents. 'Laura, would you mind very much if I go on ahead while you wait with Tariq and Skye? There seems to be some confusion over our documentation. Here is your boarding pass. As soon as Rowenna gets here, say goodbye to Tariq and Skye and board the ship immediately. A steward will show you where to go. You have your phone with you, don't you? Any problems, call me on my mobile.'

He shook Tariq's hand. 'Goodbye, lad. It's a shame you can't come with us. I know that Laura will miss you. Next time. Bye, Skye. Hey, that rhymes!'

Laughing, he joined the colourful stream of passengers crossing the gangplank to the ship and soon disappeared from view.

Laura looked at Tariq. He was eleven like her and tall for his age, but when she'd first met him he'd been almost skeletally thin. Since then he'd filled out and become sinewy and strong. He had skin the colour of burnt caramel, amber eyes and glossy black hair that came down to his collar. Laura, by contrast, had a cap of pale blonde hair, grey eyes and peaches-and-cream skin. Walking down the street, they made a striking pair, particularly if the husky was with them.

'If this was a movie, I'd smuggle you and Skye on board

26

and we'd all sail away to the Caribbean together,' Laura said.

'That would be cool. I'd love that.' Tariq's tone was wistful. He'd recently learned to swim and he loved boats and the sea. 'I'm going to miss you.'

The husky whined softly. He'd been downcast ever since Laura had taken her suitcase out of the cupboard. He didn't understand why he couldn't go to Antigua too.

Laura scanned the crowds. There was no sign of Rowenna. A gleam came into her eye. 'Tariq, I have an idea. Why don't you come aboard with me and you can take a quick look around the ship. There's plenty of time before it sails.'

Tariq's face lit up. 'Really?'

'Really.'

'But what about Rowenna? Won't she be worried if she comes back and doesn't see me?'

'She'll probably guess you're on the *Ocean Empress*. Besides, you're likely to be back before she is. She can always call us if she's anxious.'

With that, the trio joined the throng of holidaymakers, many of whom were wearing shorts, flip-flops, sunglasses and great flopping beach hats in defiance of the scudding grey clouds, whipping wind and churning sea. As they crossed the gangplank, Laura felt more cheerful than she had in days. In moments, she'd be on board the *Ocean Empress* and on her way to the Caribbean. Nothing could stop her now.

She'd have been less happy had she known that, at the precise minute she was presenting her boarding pass to the steward, a man on the jetty was following her progress with binoculars. Had she known who he was, she'd have wondered what the stranger Calvin Redfern had met with in the dead of Thursday night in St Ives' cemetery was doing at Falmouth Harbour at eight on a Sunday morning.

As Laura stepped onto the ship, he took out his mobile and barked four short words into it: 'The game has begun.'

5

'**WHERE'S YOUR BOARDING PASS**, young man?' the steward asked Tariq, barring his way. 'And I need to see the dog's papers too.'

'They're not travelling . . .' Laura began, but the rest of her sentence was drowned out by the escalation of a row going on beside her.

'Yes, ma'am, it's true that we charge by the cabin and not by the person,' the purser was saying patiently, 'but that's based on the understanding that, since there is only one double bed, a maximum of two people can share. If you wanted a family cabin you should have asked for one.'

A woman in a white sundress that contrasted sharply with her orange tan removed her sunglasses. 'Are you telling me I have to break the heart of my ten-year-old son, Jimmy?' she demanded in a shrill voice, indicating a podgy boy with ears that stuck out like wing mirrors, a coppery dusting of freckles on his nose, and hair that made him look as if he was the victim of a recent tornado.

Jimmy, Laura noted, did not look in the least bit devastated at the possibility of being made to leave the ship. He was absent-mindedly eating an ice cream while peering at a control panel dotted with flashing lights and multi-coloured buttons. 'Dad? Dad, what do you think this does?' he asked, indicating a scarlet lever marked: 'For emergency use only.'

His father, a giant of a man in a loud Hawaiian shirt, brushed him aside and advanced on the purser. 'Let me get this straight. You want us to break the heart of our boy and wreck his dreams?'

Jimmy's right hand hovered over the lever. He had the look of someone who'd run a mile to avoid doing five minutes of sport, but his small, bright brown eyes were alive with curiosity, dreaminess and mischief. Laura decided he was like a cross between a naughty cartoon character and a squirrel.

'I don't think you should touch that,' she said.

He regarded her with surprise. 'Why?'

Laura was taken aback. Usually it was she who questioned everything, especially rules and orders, and it was odd to have the tables turned on her.

'Because,' she retorted. That was the favourite response of grown ups who didn't know the answer but wanted to pretend that they did.

'Because why?'

Beside her, Tariq coughed to hide a laugh.

'I just don't think it's a very good idea, that's all.'

Jimmy licked his ice cream. 'Oh.'

Laura and Tariq turned their attention back to the row, which was heating up. 'Sir, ma'am, I'm not telling you which of you should be disappointed,' the purser was saying to Jimmy's parents. 'What I am telling you is – '

Laura was quite interested to see what would happen next, but she could feel the boy's gaze boring into her. '*What?*'

He shrugged. 'I was just wondering if you and your friend were in trouble with the law.'

Tariq was incredulous. 'Do we look like criminals?'

Laura was unable to prevent a hot flush of guilt stealing up her neck. Had Jimmy overheard them talking on the dock? Did he know that Tariq and Skye were not supposed to be on board?

'Don't be ridiculous,' she said crossly. 'Why would you say a thing like that?'

Jimmy gestured towards the crowded jetty with his ice cream, which had sprung a leak and now left a trail of green across his T-shirt. 'Then why were you being watched by a sinister man with binoculars?'

'What sinister man? What on earth are you going on about? Is this your idea of a joke? Leave us alone and don't talk to us any more. Oh, and you might want to do

31

something about your ice cream before it totally destroys the carpet.'

'I want to see a supervisor!' Jimmy's father was ranting.

'Is this going to take all day?' demanded another passenger, waiting to board. There were murmurs of discontent from others in the queue.

The purser turned away and, in a whisper, asked the steward to call security in case things got ugly. Rolling his eyes at Tariq and Laura, he said: 'Go ahead, kids. This might take a while.' He checked Laura's boarding pass. 'Deck C, you're on. Through that door and down two flights of stairs. Cabin 126.'

As he prepared to face the family once more, Laura heard him mutter: 'Where's a good tidal wave when you need one?'

Laura was very proud of Skye, who throughout this exchange had sat regally beside her. She gave him a big pat as she and Tariq ducked into the stairwell.

They were halfway down the first set of steps when the boat horn sounded and a message came over the tannoy: 'Will all visitors and personnel not travelling on the *Ocean Empress* today please leave the ship immediately.'

Laura's phone started ringing. It was Rowenna panicking about the whereabouts of Tariq. 'Oh, no,' said Laura, unable to bear the thought of saying farewell to her best friend and her beloved husky. 'I really wanted to show you around the ship, Tariq. That annoying family delayed us.'

Tariq hesitated. 'We're almost at your cabin. Maybe there's still time for me to take a quick look inside.'

Laura snatched at the chance of a temporary reprieve. 'Oh, I'm sure there is. It's only going to take a second.' She sent Rowenna's call through to Voicemail. 'Come on, let's hurry.'

At the top of the next set of stairs, however, they were forced to slow. The light wasn't working properly. It flickered on and off and snap, crackled and popped alarmingly. Laura hoped it was not about to burst into flames.

The crackling stopped abruptly and they were plunged into darkness, Laura gripped the banister with one hand and Skye's lead with the other. It was silly, she knew, but she felt a bit nervous. She was glad Tariq was right behind her.

Light bathed the stairwell. A person lay sprawled on the floor of the corridor. Before she could make out whether they were dead or alive, the blackness descended. 'Did you see that?' she whispered to Tariq, not sure why she was whispering.

'I know what I think I saw, but I'm really hoping I'm mistaken.'

The boat horn sounded. The step beneath Laura's feet rocked slightly. 'Tariq, you need to go,' she said into the darkness.

'There's no way I'm leaving you until I know everything is okay.'

The light flickered on and Laura gave a cry. Lying at the foot of the stairs was her uncle. Skye bounded forward. Laura and Tariq rushed too, almost falling down the remaining stairs when blackness swallowed them again.

As soon as the light crackled on, they flew to Calvin Redfern's side. He was unconscious. His feet were twisted at odd angles and in the space between his trouser bottoms and socks his ankles had already swollen to twice their normal size. The husky licked his face.

A sob escaped Laura.

Calvin Redfern stirred. Wincing at the pain, he pushed Skye away and stared up at them groggily. 'Where am I?'

'On the ship – the *Ocean Empress,*' Laura told him. 'You've had a bad fall. Uncle, Tariq and Skye will stay with you. I'm going to get help.'

'No!' With surprising strength and speed, his hand shot out and grabbed her wrist. 'No help and no doctors. No one must know. Promise me.'

In the instant before the light fizzled out again, Laura caught Tariq's eye. He looked as startled as she was. 'I promise,' she said, not feeling as if she had any choice.

Her uncle squeezed her hand. 'Thank you.'

The corridor flooded with light. Calvin Redfern struggled to sit up. His eyes widened as it dawned on him that not everyone present was meant to be there. 'What on earth are you doing on the ship, Tariq? You're supposed to be meeting Rowenna on the jetty. Laura, what's going on? Why is Skye here?'

'Umm, well, you said not to leave Tariq on his own . . .' Laura stammered. 'I was about to show him our cabin. Everything would have been all right if it wasn't for—'

'But where the devil is Rowenna?' Calvin Redfern demanded, his voice rising.

His phone trilled in his pocket. As he reached for it

there was a sudden, violent jolt. Laura had never been on a cruise ship in her life, but there was no mistaking the motion. The *Ocean Empress* had just set sail for the Caribbean.

6

'**CALM DOWN, ROWENNA.** Calm down. Everything is fine. Tariq is safely here with us. Skye is on board too. Yes, I know the ship has set sail. Believe me, I'm all too aware of that. I'm terribly sorry for the short notice, but there's been a last minute change of plan. Tariq and Skye will be coming on holiday with us after all. Would you mind getting in touch with Tariq's foster parents and letting them know when we'll be back. In the meantime, why don't you enjoy a well-earned break? You certainly deserve it.'

Calvin Redfern hung up, mouth set in a grim line. 'I'm trying hard not to be furious with the pair of you. What were you thinking? How am I going to explain to the captain that the *Ocean Empress* has ended up with a couple of stowaways?'

Footsteps rang on the steps above. Before they could answer, he said quickly: 'Never mind about that now. I need your help to get back to my cabin.'

He tried to stand and collapsed with a yelp, his face grey with pain.

Laura was worried sick. She regretted promising not to go for help.

Tariq, who'd promised nothing, said: 'Sir, please let me call a doctor.'

'No!' Calvin Redfern's face was contorted with pain, but he was adamant. 'You have to give me your word, both of you. I feel foolish enough as it is without being made to feel like an invalid by some over-zealous ship's quack. Nothing he or she could do anyway. Rest is the best cure. Let's say no more about it. Now, could you possibly lend me a hand?'

With the aid of Tariq, Laura and especially Skye, who he used as a furry crutch, he managed to half crawl, half drag himself into cabin 135. It was every bit as luxurious as the brochure promised, its walls papered in baby blue. A navy and white candy-striped duvet cover lent a nautical touch to the bed. There was a lamp with a ship in a bottle for a base, and, beside the porthole window, a print of a yacht on high seas.

The children helped Calvin Redfern remove his boots – a distressing job because it was agony for him – and eased him onto the bed. While Laura arranged his pillows and made him as comfortable as she could, Tariq followed his instructions on treating severely sprained ankles.

'Put a pillow under my feet so that my – ow – ankles are above the height of my heart. Thanks, Tariq. Now take a small towel from the bathroom. See that fridge over there? Check if there's any ice in it. There is? Miracles never cease. Right, empty an icetray into the towel, wrap up the cubes and rest the whole thing on my ankles. The ice will help the swelling to go down. Thanks, son. You've done a great job.'

Tariq glowed with pride. He had the greatest possible respect for Calvin Redfern, to whom he felt he owed his life, and was wracked with guilt that he'd made him angry and caused him anxiety by coming aboard the ship.

Calvin Redfern collapsed into his pillows, beads of sweat on his upper lip. 'Laura,' he said weakly, 'would you be kind enough to look in the front pocket of my suitcase? You'll find a First Aid kit in there. A couple of painkillers and a glass of water would be very welcome right now.'

Mission accomplished, Laura was finally able to ask: 'Uncle Calvin, how did you manage to sprain both ankles? What happened?'

'An accident, pure and simple. I was on my way down the steps when the passage light went off and I was plunged into darkness. Unfortunately, I was in mid-step at the time. My foot caught on a carpet string or something and I tripped. That's the last I remember until I woke up with Skye licking my face.'

He grimaced. 'Good thing I have a whole week to recover before we get to the Caribbean. I'm really sorry, Laura, but I'm likely to be laid up and no fun at all for the best part of the voyage.'

Laura hugged him. 'Don't worry about anything except getting better. We'll go now and let you sleep. Call if you need us.'

'Not so fast,' ordered her uncle in the closest he ever came to a stern tone. 'I'm still waiting for an explanation from the pair of you. Have you any idea how much trouble we're in? How are we going to afford to pay for Tariq's cruise, accommodation and flights, Laura? What are the Antigua authorities going to say when we turn up with a dog with no papers and a boy with no passport, Tariq? I suspect that we'll be put on the next flight home. Holiday over.'

Laura's eyes filled with tears. 'I'm so sorry, Uncle Calvin. It was my idea that Tariq have a look at my cabin and this is all my fault.'

Tariq interrupted: 'No, it was *my* idea and it's *my* fault. Laura was only trying to do something nice for me because she knew how badly I wanted to see the ship. Punish me, but please don't be mad at Laura.'

'Actually,' Calvin Redfern said, trying to hide a smile, 'it's my fault. If you hadn't stopped to help me, Tariq, you'd more than likely have made it off the ship.'

Tariq said suddenly, 'I've just thought of something. I have my new British passport with me. It arrived last week and my foster parents told me to keep it with me for the holidays in case I needed it for identity or something. It's in my backpack, with all my clothes.'

Laura sniffed and said: 'Well, at least we won't be deported from Antigua. We'll only be jailed for helping two stowaways.'

'I don't suppose you have a few thousand pounds in your backpack, Tariq?' Calvin Redfern asked, only half joking.

There was a moment of glum silence, and then Laura said: 'Hey, I've had a thought. Tariq, didn't the purser tell Jimmy's parents that the ship owners charged per cabin, not per person? When I won the competition, my uncle and I thought we'd be sharing a cabin. Now it turns out we have one each. Uncle Calvin, would it be okay if Tariq and Skye stayed with me – at least until we get to Antigua?'

The painkillers were taking effect and Calvin Redfern's voice was thick with tiredness. 'Good thinking, Laura. I did read something about that in the brochure but didn't take any notice of it at the time because, like you, I thought we'd be sharing a cabin. Yes, it's absolutely fine for Tariq to stay with you because you're in a twin room with two beds. Pass me that folder on the dresser. I'll check the hotel details for Antigua.'

A minute later he looked up. 'We have a three-bedroom villa to ourselves so there'll be no problem there.'

He ran a weary hand over his eyes. 'Well, that's a relief. There's still Tariq's air ticket back to London to think about, but we'll worry about that later. From memory, I have thousands of unused Air Miles I earned through work that might take care of it. Now all we have to worry about is one very large husky. We can't exactly hide him. He'll go mad if he can't exercise. Laura, when you rescued Skye, were you given any documents for him?'

'Loads. I have his pedigree papers, his rabies and vaccination certificates, his pet passport. . .'

'His pet passport?' interrupted her uncle. 'Why didn't you say that in the first place?'

'I've only just thought of it. Besides, it's sitting in my bedroom at Ocean View Terrace. It's not much use to us there.'

'No, but we can email Rowenna and get her to scan it and send it to us. It may be that he's covered for the Caribbean. If so, our problem is solved. Not' – he put his cross face on – 'that you deserve to have got off so lightly.'

'Sorry,' said Laura.

'Sorry,' added Tariq, looking sheepish.

'Having said that, now that we have a plan and things seem to be working out, may I say how happy I am that you're with us, Tariq – and you, Skye – especially since Laura is going to need the company.'

'Thanks, Mr Redfern.' Tariq gave him a huge smile. 'I'm pretty happy about it too.'

'So am I,' added Laura fervently.

They really did leave then, because her uncle's eyelids were drooping and Laura wanted him to rest and forget for a while how a broken stairwell light had ruined his voyage. She wondered if he had grounds to sue.

When they emerged from his cabin, however, they saw that the light was working perfectly. So perfectly that there was no mistaking the Hawaiian beachwear of the man and woman barrelling noisily down the corridor, their son trailing behind. Laura thought he had a lonely air about him, but when he spotted her and Tariq he gave them a cheeky grin.

'Daylight robbery is what I call it,' his mother was

ranting. 'Wait till I get back home. That travel agent's life won't be worth living.'

Laura groaned. 'Just our luck to be on the same deck as them.'

'Don't worry about it,' Tariq reassured her. 'It's such a massive ship, this will probably be the last we ever see of them.'

It was only when Laura unlocked the door to their cabin that she cast aside the worries of the past few days and her spirits truly lifted. While cabin 126 was a mirror image of her uncle's in terms of decoration, it also had doors opening out onto a balcony, beyond which a limitless stretch of ocean was visible. Skye rushed over to the railings and barked at the flying spray.

Laura's whole being flooded with happiness. Despite everything the Fates had done to prevent it she was on board a luxury cruise liner, heading for the Caribbean. Best of all, Tariq and Skye were with her. They were in the middle of the sea. What could possibly go wrong?

7

LAURA'S DETECTIVE HERO, Matt Walker, had a saying: If something seems too good to be true it usually is. But she'd not found that to be the case with the ship at all. If anything, the *Ocean Empress* exceeded her expectations by about a thousand per cent.

There were so many forms of entertainment they made her head spin. On that first afternoon, when she and Tariq had explored every corner of the cruise liner, they were like kids let loose in a chocolate bazaar. Especially since they'd discovered that everything really was free – or, at least included in the prize. That meant they could try anything, do anything, or eat anything they liked.

After a delicious lunch of chips slathered with ketchup and ice cream sundaes piled high with honeycomb, banana, chocolate sprinkles and marshmallows, they went from deck to deck, mapping out their days.

'We could have seafood tonight, curry tomorrow and fish and chips on Wednesday,' suggested Tariq. 'And maybe because the weather is still a bit grey and blowy, we should go ice-skating this afternoon? I've never tried it before. There weren't a lot of ice rinks in Bangladesh.'

'Ice-skating on a ship – sounds brilliant!' agreed Laura. 'How about going to the water park if it's sunny tomorrow morning, followed by . . . ooh, I don't know, nine holes of miniature golf. If you're feeling brave, we could try the rock climbing wall on Wednesday.'

Tariq laughed. 'We could have ice cream sundaes every day and in the evenings we could try the whirlpool, the sauna, or the theatre.'

Laura giggled. 'How will we fit it all in?' Then she felt a twinge of guilt. 'Poor uncle Calvin. It's so unfair that we get to enjoy ourselves while he's trapped in his cabin.'

'It is unfair,' agreed Tariq, 'but my foster father says that sometimes injuries or illnesses are nature's way of telling people to slow down. Your uncle seems pretty exhausted from work. Besides, he'll have lots of fun in Antigua.'

Laura smiled. 'You could be right. He did look pretty happy when we took him the ice cream sundae, and it was a bonus finding the latest Matt Walker book in the gift shop. He could hardly wait for us to leave so he could start it.'

The highlight of the afternoon was when a pod of

dolphins appeared. At the time Laura and Tariq were standing on a viewing point on the prow of the ship watching as the world they knew gave way to a shifting landscape of bold, dark blue. It parted before the white bow of the *Ocean Empress,* throwing up diamond droplets.

Laura looked down and felt almost giddy. Below that silken surface were marine worlds as teeming with life as London, New York or Rome. Thousands of leagues beneath the sea, there were creatures as enigmatic as the giant squid. There were sharks with mouths as big as doors. There were forests of pulsing coral and shipwrecks and navy submarines. And yet none of it was visible. The uniform blue of the sea was like a theatre curtain, hiding a performance.

Occasionally that curtain lifted to reveal a glimpse of the spectacle below. If whales and seals are the actors of the ocean, dolphins are the acrobats. Out of the blue, twelve of them soared to the surface on the crest of a wave and began racing the ship, performing somersaults and gravity-defying leaps at astonishing speed. They ducked and dived like quicksilver. Watching them, it was quite impossible not to feel happy. They were in love with life; glorying in their strength and freedom.

Afterwards, Laura and Tariq tried ice-skating. It was hard to say which of them was worse than the other and they spent most of the time in a heap on the ice, laughing until their sides hurt. There was something quite surreal about trying to skate on a ship rolling on the Atlantic. It was very entertaining.

By dinnertime, they'd worked up an enormous appetite,

which they'd decided could only be satisfied by an equally enormous seafood platter. First, though, they'd checked on Calvin Redfern. A room service waiter had brought him the cheeseburger Laura had ordered for him, but it lay untouched. He was fast asleep.

Laura filled up his water glass and smoothed the cover over him, her heart contracting. Under normal circumstances, her uncle exuded strength. It distressed her to see him looking so vulnerable.

'He'll be as good as new before you know it,' Tariq said gently. 'He's like a sleeping lion. It won't be long before he roars again.'

Laura smiled. A sleeping lion was a lovely image. Tariq was right. Calvin Redfern would be stronger than ever in no time.

It was early when they walked into the Happy Clam but already it was buzzing. There was another seafood restaurant with starched tablecloths, shiny wine glasses and waiters dressed in black and white, but it hadn't been inviting at all. The Happy Clam looked much more friendly. It had rustic wooden tables, red-checked tablecloths and a buffet groaning with prawns, lobsters, oysters and so many species of fish Laura marvelled that there were any left in the sea.

She and Tariq loaded their plates with garlic prawns, rice and big chunks of lemon and settled down at an empty table. It was delicious food and they positively beamed as they tucked into it. Unfortunately, their peace was soon shattered. Five minutes after they sat down, the volume in the restaurant rose by several decibels. When they glanced up, Jimmy's parents were bearing down on them. Their son had proceeded directly to the buffet table, where he was wresting a lobster with claws as big as spades onto his plate.

'You don't mind if we join you, do you?' cried his mum, plonking herself down beside Laura. 'The posh restaurant claimed to be full, which I'm certain was a blatant lie, and now this place is crammed to the gills.'

Bob thrust out a meaty paw. 'Bob and Rita Gannet, how do you do?'

Laura rescued her hand and discreetly wiped it on her napkin under the table. 'I'm Laura and this is Tariq.'

Bob flagged down a waiter. 'Two beers, two tropical juices, and two fish and chips with all the trimmings.'

The waiter opened his mouth as if to protest that the whole point of a buffet restaurant was that customers served themselves, thought better of it, and grunted assent.

Jimmy returned with a towering platter. Rita introduced him to Laura and Tariq, but his cheeks were stuffed with lobster and although he nodded and mumbled a greeting he avoided their eyes.

'Where are your parents, kids?' asked Rita, squeezing ketchup onto her chips. 'At the theatre? In the casino?'

Laura opened her mouth to say that they were with her uncle who was lying injured in his cabin, but he was such an intensely private man and so loathed being an invalid

47

that it felt almost as if she'd be betraying him. 'We're travelling alone,' she said.

Tariq looked at her in surprise. So did the Gannets.

'What, without a guardian?' Rita wanted to know.

'Not exactly.' Laura admitted. 'We're with my uncle but not with him, if you see what I mean.'

Bob chuckled and waggled a chip at her. 'I get it. He's wearing an invisibility cloak!'

Laura had to make an effort not to roll her eyes. 'No, that's not it at all. He's real and he is on the ship, it's just that he's under deep cover.'

'That's right,' said Tariq, not quite sure where she was going with this, but willing to support her all the same. And so far everything was true. Calvin Redern *was* deep under cover – the bed cover.

Jimmy gave up trying to pretend he wasn't remotely interested in them and sat up in his chair. His lobster was forgotten.

Rita smiled indulgently. 'You mean, like a spy?'

'No, I mean he's a detective,' Laura told her. 'He used to be – ' she corrected herself – 'still is, one of the best in the world. As good as Matt Walker. Matt's a fictional detective, but he's so brilliant he might as well be real. He's real to me.'

'So lemme get this shhtraight,' said Bob, his words muffled by a mouthful of fish. 'Your uncle who is not here really is here, and Matt Walker, whoever he is, is not real but you think he is, and both of them are detectives?'

'Umm . . . I suppose so, yes.'

'Who is he hunting?' Jimmy said, pushing his plate

away. 'Your uncle, I mean. Who's he after? Is it something to do with the sinister man with the binoculars?'

'*What* sinister man?' Bob wanted to know.

'Jimmy, sweetheart, if there's a scary stranger on the ship, I want to know about it,' Rita said anxiously. Her voice rose. 'How many times have I warned you about stranger danger?'

'There is no sinister man, Mrs Gannet,' Laura said. 'He's making it up.'

'He often does that,' Rita told her. 'Jimmy, are you telling stories again?'

Jimmy scowled. 'Am not.'

Laura scowled back. 'Okay, what did he look like?'

'Weird. I only noticed him because everyone on the dock was smiling or excited or busy and he was like a stiff black insect, staring.'

Beneath the table, Laura's skin suddenly crawled as if a hundred beetles were marching across it. Tariq went still in his chair. The image was too specific to be invented.

Laura thought of her uncle, laid up in his cabin. It was bad enough that he had two sprained ankles, but his fall could have been so much worse. What if it hadn't been an accident? But, no, that was impossible. He'd tripped going down the steps because he was in a hurry. Not even the Straight A gang could have organised that.

'Even if there was a weird man – and I'm not saying there was – he would hardly have been looking at me and Tariq,' she told Jimmy. 'We're two ordinary kids enjoying a holiday with our uncle.'

'Your *detective* uncle,' he pointed out. 'Detectives have

lots of enemies. Anyway, you still haven't told us why he's under cover.'

And I'm not going to, you annoying little brat, Laura wanted to say, but she stabbed a roll with her butter knife instead.

'Are there criminals walking around the ship?' Jimmy persisted.

'Ooh, I do hope not,' said Rita, looking at the queue for the buffet counter as if she expected any murderers and thieves to be wearing placards.

'Don't be a dodo,' boomed Bob, pounding a paw on the table. The salt and pepper leapt into the air. 'As if they'd allow criminals on the *Ocean Empress*.'

Several people glanced their way and a woman at the next table giggled nervously.

Laura couldn't believe she'd been so stupid as to say that her uncle was a detective, much less than he was under cover. If she'd said he was a little under the weather, they'd have imagined he was seasick and the whole conversation would have been over by now.

'Besides,' Bob was saying, 'I think they're making it up. It's pure fantasy.'

Tariq had been silent throughout, but now he sat up. 'Sir, if there's one thing Laura never does, it's lie. She's too loyal to her uncle to tell you, but the truth is he's not very well at the moment and is unable to join us for meals. However, he was once a brilliant detective and Laura takes after him. She's a pretty fine investigator herself. She'll be as good as Matt Walker when she's older.'

'I'm going to be a detective too,' announced Jimmy. He'd been tucking into a trifle and had a cream moustache with chocolate sprinkles. 'Only I'm going to be even better than Matt Walker. And fifty times better than your invisible uncle.'

Laura had an overwhelming desire to leap across the table and shove his face in his trifle. 'I bet you don't even know who Matt Walker is,' she said scornfully.

'Do too.'

'Don't.'

'Do.'

Rita wiped her mouth on her napkin and put an arm around her son. 'But honey, only yesterday you were telling us you wanted to be a submarine commander. And before that you said your dream was to be an engineer and build a skyscraper.'

Jimmy shoved an enormous portion of trifle into his mouth, smiled angelically and said: 'Well, now I'm going to be the best detective in the world!'

'Of course you are, hon,' smiled Rita. To the other children she said: 'He's very bright, our Jimmy. Top of the class he is in every subject. Loves science and maths, don't you, sweetie?'

Bob signalled to the waiter to bring him a portion of lemon meringue pie from the dessert counter. 'Laura, Tariq, I apologise for doubting you. Clearly you and your mysterious uncle are not to be trifled with. Trifle – get it, tee hee. Better still, you obviously have a lot in common with my son, so you'll have lots to chat about over the next week or so. How nice, Jimmy, that you have two new friends.'

As soon as they were outside, Laura put her hands over her face and let out a muffled scream. 'Two new friends! Lots to chat about during the voyage! They've got to be kidding.'

'It's a big ship,' said Tariq. 'Hopefully we'll never see them again.'

'That's what you said this morning and we've just had to suffer through an entire dinner with them. As if that aggravating boy could be a better detective than Uncle Calvin. *Fifty times* better! I couldn't believe my ears.'

'Maybe he thought it was a way to make us like him – to say he wanted to be a detective. He seems lonely. I know he's a bit irritating, but maybe we should give him a chance. You were kind to me when I was the loneliest boy on earth, and that turned out to be the best thing that ever happened to me.'

'Yes, but you were the nicest, bravest, most wonderful person I'd ever met, and he's . . . he's the most infuriating.' She stopped. 'Don't look at me like that, Tariq.'

He grinned. 'Like what?'

'With that look that makes me feel as if I'd walk across hot coals if you asked me to.'

'This look.' He put on his wounded fawn expression.

She couldn't help giggling. 'I'm absolutely not promising anything, but . . . oh, all right, I'll think about it.'

Laura was still smiling when they reached the stairs to Deck C. She was about to start down the steps when she noticed a small hook in the wall level with the second step, at around ankle height. There was a matching one on the other side.

52

That got her thinking. Her uncle had fallen because he'd tripped in the darkness on what he thought was a loose carpet string. Only trouble was, there was no carpet on the steps. There was just steel and a strip of industrial rubber that was well secured and highly unlikely to be the cause of two sprained ankles.

The hooks made Laura suspicious. They reminded her of Matt Walker's first case: *The Rocking Horse Mystery*. He'd investigated the death of a millionaire businessman who'd fallen and hit his head on a marble fireplace in a seemingly empty room. It turned out that a rival had set up a tripwire – a strand of near invisible fishing line secured between two armchairs at ankle-height. It was designed to topple the man in the exact spot where he was likely to do himself most damage.

In order for someone to do the same thing to Calvin Redfern, they'd have had to hide nearby so that the tripwire didn't kill or injure anybody else. On the right side of the stairwell was a narrow, dark space just wide enough to accommodate a very slim man. Or a woman.

Tariq looked up at her. 'Is everything all right?'

Laura skipped down the remaining stairs and unlocked the cabin. She was allowing her imagination to get the better of her. Thousands of people took tumbles down steps every year without imagining it involved a hidden assassin.

She smiled. 'I'm fine. How about we take Skye on deck and try to make friends with a waiter or chef? I'd like to find him a nice juicy bone for his dinner.'

8

FOR A SIBERIAN HUSKY like Skye, genetically programmed to run through snow for hours at a stretch, pulling heavy sledges, a cruise ship was not the best environment. Laura spent a lot of the first day worrying about how he was going to cope with being cooped up in a cabin with only a limited amount of exercise in the mornings and evenings. Until, that is, she met Fernando.

Fernando was a waiter who seemed to spend more time smoking on deck than carrying trays, but he was dog crazy. When Laura and Tariq showed up at the galley door looking for a bone for Skye, he went into raptures over the husky.

'Oh my,' he said, palms pressed to his cheeks, 'never did I think I would have such a lucky day as this. A Siberian husky – a champion among dogs – on board the *Ocean Empress*. Oh my, life suddenly looks very much brighter.'

Not only did he immediately rush away to fetch Skye a T-bone steak, he had an exercise solution – one he used with his own greyhound back in New York.

Laura couldn't believe what she was hearing. 'A treadmill?'

'You mean, one of those running machines in a gym?' Tariq asked.

Fernando grinned. 'Wait till you see for yourself.'

It turned out that the manager of the ship gym was his best friend and glad to assist them. As soon as Fernando had finished his shift, he introduced everyone and showed Laura how to train Skye to use the treadmill. At first, the husky was scared of the noise the machine made, but in no time at all he was sprinting along as if he were competing in the Iditarod Trail Sled Dog Race in Alaska. He caused quite a sensation among the other passengers. Fernando was very impressed.

'You'd never know he only had three legs. He'd give Mattie, my greyhound, a run for her money and she's like a pocket rocket.'

He was so taken with Skye and Skye with him that Laura agreed right away when he begged her to allow him to exercise the husky in his free time.

'This is the thing that will save my sanity. Otherwise all I do is miss Mattie and get bored. Nothing to look forward to but ocean, more ocean and more ocean.'

Laura found it extraordinary that anyone could get bored on the floating city that was the *Ocean Empress*, where it was possible to try half a dozen different activities and eat in a different restaurant every day of the cruise.

On their third day at sea, a Tuesday, she and Tariq spent the morning playing mini golf and chatting to her uncle. Lunch was a fudge sundae for each of them. They'd had so many pancakes for breakfast they couldn't fit in anything else.

In the afternoon, the last of the clouds blew away and a silky blue sky arched over the ship. Sea birds wheeled overhead. Passengers in bikinis and board shorts baked on sun loungers, sipping exotic cocktails with umbrellas in them.

Laura and Tariq had a lovely time shooting down water slides and kayaking along fake rapids. It was a relief to know that Skye was happy and taken care of. Calvin Redfern had woken that morning in a lot of pain, but for now he was engrossed in his Matt Walker book and finding comfort in a large chocolate cake.

'It's funny how life can change in the blink of an eye,' Tariq said. He was thinking of his nightmarish existence as a modern day slave before a chance encounter had brought him into contact with Laura.

Laura turned over onto her stomach so she could watch the activity in the wave pool from beneath the brim of her baseball cap. 'Yes, it is. We're pretty lucky.' She was thinking of how, in just a few months, she'd gone from a dreary orphanage, where she'd been bored half to death and had nothing in common with anyone, to a

Caribbean cruise ship adventure with her best friends.

From the other side of the pool came a screech that ended in a gurgle. Jimmy Gannet had exuberantly dive-bombed an inflatable dinosaur, not realising until he was in mid-air that there was a small girl floating dreamily on its back. His mum and dad rushed to inspect the damage. From a distance, they resembled a pair of excitable parrots.

'Every silver lining has a cloud,' quipped Laura.

'Tariq! Laura! My dear children, how are you?' cried Rita Gannet. She came rushing over, leaving Bob to deal with the irate mother of the crying girl. 'Oh my goodness, we simply could not stop talking about you and your uncle after you left last night,' she said, whipping off sunglasses the size of small planets. 'Jimmy's imagination has been quite fired up by it. I've never seen him so excited by anything.'

Laura fought the urge to run away. Jimmy's father had fished him out of the pool and was escorting him in their direction, wrapped in a huge flowery towel.

'Are you sure she's okay, Dad?' he was saying. 'I feel terrible. I didn't see her there.'

'Sure she is, son. Some people have nothing better to do than complain, that's all,' complained Bob, striding over and flopping down on a candy-striped lounger. The lounger collapsed in the middle, trapping him in its the depths like a Venus flytrap swallowing a bug.

Tariq, Rita and Jimmy rushed to help, but most of Laura's energy went on trying to stop a fit of giggles. In the end, she had to stuff a corner of towel into her mouth.

'Damn this cheap and nasty pool furniture,' Bob

mumbled when he finally crawled scarlet and sweaty from the clutches of the chair. 'Rita, add that to the list of things we've found wrong so far, and we'll try to get some money back.'

'Yes, dear,' said his wife. 'How are you enjoying the ship so far, kids? Is your uncle on the mend, Laura? What's wrong with him, anyway? Is he seasick?'

'He's much better, thank you,' responded Laura, ignoring the question.

'Great, great. And what are your plans for tomorrow?'

Laura glanced quickly at Tariq. She knew what was coming next. The Gannets wanted a playmate for Jimmy. She wracked her brains for an excuse. 'Well, we hadn't decided . . . We're not sure . . .'

Then she remembered Tariq's words. She knew he was right, they should give Jimmy a chance. 'Actually, we were thinking of trying the rock climbing wall.'

Bob poked his son. 'Rock climbing! Awesome. You'd love that, son, wouldn't you? Didn't you once say that you dreamed of being a mountaineer?'

'Dad, Tariq and Laura don't want me hanging round and anyway I'd rather be with you and Mum.'

'Nonsense,' retorted his father. 'They don't mind at all, do you kids? The more the merrier. It'll be fun for you to be with children your own age.'

'You'd be very welcome, Jimmy,' Tariq said politely. 'We'd be glad to have you along.'

'See, what did I tell you?' Bob boomed, clapping Jimmy on the back. 'Now how about it, son? It'll give you a chance to discuss all that detective stuff with Laura.'

'Can't think of anything I'd like more,' Laura said insincerely.

Jimmy looked as if he'd rather stand knee-deep in a tankful of piranhas, but he gave a weak smile and said, 'Sure, Dad. That would be great.'

'Fantastic,' said Rita. 'It's a date.'

~ 9 ~

'WE'RE DOING THE rock climbing with him and that's it,'
Laura told Tariq as they headed back to their cabin after
taking Skye for his early morning walk on Wednesday.
'There's no way I'm having Jimmy Gannet hanging around
and ruining our whole holiday. He's a disaster waiting to
happen, that boy.'

She stopped. 'What is it, Skye?'

The husky had halted abruptly at their cabin door,
hackles raised.

'It's probably the cleaner,' Tariq said, nodding at
the housekeeping trolley parked two doors down, but
he hesitated before slipping his key card into the lock.

'That's weird, the door has been locked from the inside.'

Laura pushed past the growling husky and knocked hard. 'Is anyone in there?'

'Don't tell me you've forgotten your key as well?' demanded a pink-faced maid, emerging from cabin 130. 'You kids! What am I going to do with you?' She had a cheerful smile and a roly-poly figure all but sewn into her blue and white uniform.

Laura placed a warning hand on Skye's collar. The hairs stood up on the back of her neck. For some reason, Jimmy's words about the 'insect' man watching them board the ship came into her head. 'As well as what?'

The maid unlocked the door with a master key. 'As well as your young brother. Now don't forget it again, because I'm leaving now and have the rest of the day off.'

Skye almost wrenched Laura's arm from its socket, so keen was he to burst into the cabin. But his growl soon changed to a whine. Stretched out on Laura's bed, reading her Matt Walker book and listening to the iPod Tariq had been given for his birthday, was Jimmy.

Far from appearing embarrassed to be caught in their cabin, Jimmy grinned at their expressions. It was barely nine o'clock but already he looked as if he'd been through a wind tunnel. His hair was sticking up in all directions and there was ketchup on his shirt.

'Hello, Laura and Tariq and big wolf dog,' he said,

removing the headphones from his ears. 'Surprised to see me? I must say that, for a detective, you're pretty lax about your security, Laura.' He held up the book. 'I don't think Matt Walker would approve.'

Laura snatched it from him. She was trembling with fury. 'What do you think you're playing at, Jimmy Gannet? Or is this normal behaviour for you? Are you in the habit of breaking into people's rooms and going through their things? Do you realise that we could call security and have you arrested?'

Jimmy propped himself up on the bed and regarded her with amusement. 'You get all red when you're cross. Now that I've decided to be an ace detective myself, I wanted to see how easy it would be to get inside a locked room. And it was. Very easy. It only took about two minutes.'

'But why our cabin?' asked Tariq. 'Couldn't you have experimented with your parents' cabin or something?'

Jimmy said coolly: 'Where's the challenge in that? Anyway I was hoping to meet your famous uncle. Where is he anyway? Hiding under the bed?'

Laura glared at him. 'So how *did* you get in?'

He snorted. 'Easy as pie, wasn't it. I told the cleaner that I'd locked myself out and that I couldn't find my mum or my sister, and she let me in straight away. Well, I'm a kid, aren't I? She's not going to think that a ten-year-old is going to make up a story like that – not on a fancy cruise ship. She did ask me if I had any ID, and I told her that the best proof I could give her was that she'd definitely find a Matt Walker book in the cabin. And sure enough, there was.'

Tariq laughed. 'That is pretty gutsy.'

'No, it's not,' Laura said indignantly. 'It's called breaking and entering. I'm going to call security.' She reached for the phone and began to dial.

Instantly Jimmy's bravado crumpled. A minute ago, he'd seemed much older, wiser and more confident than his ten years, but now he just was a scared kid. He sat up and hugged his knees, one of which was badly grazed. It had two crossed plasters on it. Tears brimmed in his eyes but he blinked them away.

'Oh, please don't do that. Please. Dad will cause a scene and it'll be hugely embarrassing. Look, I'm sorry. I didn't mean to offend you. I just . . .'

'You just what?' demanded Laura. 'You just thought you'd steal my book, help yourself to Tariq's iPod and frighten the life out of us?'

Jimmy picked at the bedcover. 'I wanted to prove to you that I could be a detective too.'

Laura was not yet ready to forgive him. 'A detective fifty times as good as my uncle?'

He flushed. 'You didn't like that, I suppose.'

'There's something else, isn't there?' said Tariq.

Jimmy looked sheepish. 'I guess I wanted to see what it was like to be you for a while.'

Tariq sat down beside him. '*Us?* Why on earth would you want to be like us?'

'Well, you're best friends, aren't you? I saw you and your cool dog on the dock before you boarded the ship. We were standing quite near to you for a while. There was something about the way you were talking to each other and laughing, it was obvious that you'd do anything for each other.'

'Yes, we would,' said Laura, softening a little now that he'd praised Skye, 'but that's no excuse for breaking into our cabin.'

Jimmy hugged his knees harder. 'I've never had a friend. Not a real one. And my life is so boring compared to yours. You live by the sea and you have a husky and investigate things. Your uncle is a famous detective. My life is really, really dull and my mum and dad, I love them, right, but they're embarrassing. My dad, he's loud and makes people stare. And my mum sometimes treats me like I'm a baby.'

Laura's eyes met Tariq's. All of her anger drained away. It was true what Tariq said. You never could tell what was inside a person.

'First,' she said, 'you don't know how much Tariq and I envy you.'

Jimmy stared at her. '*Me?* Why?'

'Because you have two parents who adore you. That's worth any amount of embarrassment, trust me. Both Tariq and I are orphans. Tariq is from Bangladesh and his parents were basically worked into an early grave. My mum died when I was born and I don't know who my father was. Some people say he was an American. But that's okay because my uncle is the best person in the world and the only father I would ever want. All I'm saying is that a booming voice and being overprotected are a small price to pay for having a mum and dad who love you.

'Secondly, your life is exciting. You're on a cruise ship with dolphins jumping all around and submarines and giant squid sliding underneath, and you're about to come rock climbing with us.

'And lastly, you do have friends. You have Tariq and me. But if you ever pull a stunt like this again, we'll be ex-friends. Got it?'

A smile broke like a new day across Jimmy's face. 'Got it.'

~ 10 ~

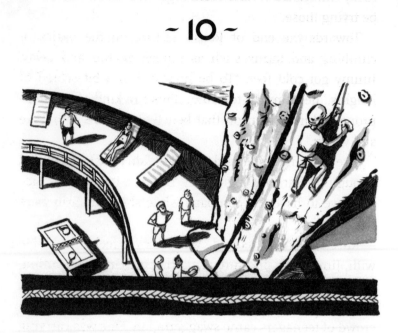

THE BIG COUNTRY adventure centre was run by a rugged instructor called Russ. His bronzed hands looked strong enough to grind golf balls to powder.

'The first three rules of rock climbing are check, double check and triple check your equipment,' he told them. 'Your ropes are your lifeline. When all else fails, you need to be able to depend on them. You won't hear us talk a lot about safety here, although nothing is more important to us. But we can't guarantee it. Any time you leave the ground it's a high-risk activity.'

Laura craned her neck to gaze up at the wall. It was the height of two decks of the ship and made to look like a real rocky cliff. It had several overhangs. She didn't think she'd be trying those.

Towards the end of Russ's lecture on the basics of climbing and terms such as rappel, anchor and belay, Jimmy got cold feet. 'To be honest, I'm a bit scared of heights,' he admitted to Laura. 'Plus I'm kind of accident-prone. I think I'll sit on that bench over there with Skye and watch.'

'Are you sure?' she said, but she didn't push it. He had enough of that from his father. Besides, it would be nice for Skye to have the company while she and Tariq were climbing.

Russ was equally relaxed. 'Whatever you feel comfortable with, Jimmy. No pressure at all. If you change your mind, let me know and we'll kit you out.'

The doors of the adventure centre burst open and a crowd of teenagers came swaggering in. One was carrying a digital radio blaring ear-splitting rock.

Russ groaned. 'Something tells me we might have a booking mix-up here,' he said. 'Bear with me, kids, while I sort this out. Laura and Tariq, grab yourself some rock shoes from that box over there and then head over to the gear store. Ernesto will sort you out with helmets and harnesses.'

The teenagers were dispersing noisily when Skye sprang up and raced over to a door beside the gear store. He began to scratch frantically at it. Jimmy rushed after him and tried, without success, to haul him back.

Laura picked up her harness and ran over, with Tariq following. 'What's going on?'

Jimmy gave up his struggle to stop the husky's desperate clawing. 'I don't know. One minute he was sitting peacefully and the next he was tearing over here. He seems agitated. What's behind that door?'

'Is gear store backroom,' answered a wiry dark man with an anxious face. 'Hi, I am Ernesto. What seem-us to be the problem?'

Laura had hold of Skye's collar and was trying to coax him away. 'My dog is convinced that something bad is lurking in there.'

Ernesto chuckled. 'The only bad thing that lurks in thees place is me. Is where I sort out the equipment and check the ropes. Nothing to interest your husky. No bones, ha ha.' He opened the door and waved grandly to Skye. 'Here, my friend, take a look if is a gonna make you feel better.'

But the store was empty. Skye rushed around sniffing, but it soon became clear that whatever - or whomever - he'd detected was long gone.

'You were meestaken,' Ernesto informed Skye. 'There is no bogey man here.' He sniffed. 'There is something strange though. What is thees smell? Is *chocolat*, no?'

'Chocolate peanuts,' said Tariq. 'It smells of chocolate peanuts. The Mukhtars used to sell them in their store.'

'Noots, of course,' agreed Ernesto. 'I no eat noots – very allergic – so is not me.' He shrugged. 'Nothing is disturb so is okay. Probably is one of those teen-agus.'

He steered Skye out of the way and went to close the door, but Laura stopped him. 'Wait. Where does that hatch go to?'

'Is for deliveries only. He go out to passage near restaurant.'

He shut the door. 'Now, let us see which of you will be best climber.'

'I will,' Jimmy said with a grin. 'I'll be the best mountaineer that's ever been, better than Edmund Hillary. He climbed Mount Everest back in 1953.'

Tariq raised an eyebrow. 'You've changed your mind about coming with us?'

Jimmy was pale but he nodded vigorously. 'As long as you let me go first.'

An hour earlier, his cheeky bravado would have made Laura want to throttle him, but now she recognised it for what it was and smiled warmly at him. 'Good for you. It takes real courage to overcome a fear of heights. Here, take my harness. Ernesto can find me another one.'

What the children didn't know about Russ, and what he didn't advertise, was that he was a former member of the SAS, had climbed Everest three times and, two decades before, had been one of the world's elite mountaineers.

Yet all of that experience was of no use to him when Jimmy Gannet reached the highest, most treacherous part of the climbing wall, sat down in his harness in preparation for being lowered back to the ground, and let out a yell of pure terror. 'My rope, I felt it slip. It's breaking, it's breaking.'

Ordinarily, Russ would have the last, and most vital person in the human chain of safety, on the ground. First in line was Tariq. He was the belayer. He had a belay device clipped to his harness and he'd been shortening the rope as Jimmy climbed. The rope went through Jimmy's harness, up to a metal loop called a karibiner at the top of the wall, which acted as an anchor, and back down to Tariq.

Jimmy had climbed without assistance, using his hands and feet. Laura had watched him with her heart in her mouth. He'd insisted on going first, despite being so scared he was trembling, but even so she worried that his mind was not on what he was doing. He'd been so affected by the chapters of the Matt Walker book he'd read that he'd been talking non-stop, pressing Laura for every detail about the detective's methods.

'What's the best ever tip you learned from Detective Inspector Walker?' he'd pressed.

It was a difficult question because Detective Inspector Walker had hundreds of ingenious tips and tricks, but Laura had finally decided that one of her favourites came from *The Case of the Missing Heiress*. Matt had observed that a common weakness of criminals in general and kidnappers in particular was that they were so preoccupied with trying to get the details right that they often overlooked the ordinary, mundane things. They messed up because they didn't notice the things that were staring them in the face.

'Like what?' Jimmy had pressed. 'Give me an example.'

But right then Russ had interrupted them. They were ready for Jimmy to climb the wall.

When Jimmy reached the top Russ had explained that he was to indicate he was ready to descend and Tariq would lower him with the help of the belay device, something which reduced a climber's weight to a couple of kilograms. Laura was second in the chain. She held the dead rope – rope that had already been paid out – and was there to help Tariq if Jimmy fell. Russ was there for professional backup. When working with children, he always held the very end of the rope so that he could step in quickly in an emergency.

Unfortunately, at the instant that Jimmy's rope was sliced through almost to its kern, as its core was known, the instructor was on the other side of the centre attending to a woman who had fainted.

'Help!' Jimmy yelled, but as he did the spindly twists of nylon that held him snapped so that only one remained. The sudden jolt caused him to pitch backwards into space.

Tariq and Laura had a split second to act. They used it. Russ was already sprinting towards them, but he'd taught them well. Before he reached them they'd halted Jimmy's fall in mid-air. The boy crashed against the wall and swung like a human pendulum, but after that they were able to lower him gently to the ground.

Back on solid earth, Ernesto examined Jimmy's ropes with incredulity. 'Is impossible, I check thees rope my-self,' he told Laura and Tariq while the ten-year-old was being treated for shock by the ship doctor. Skye, who seemed to sense that Jimmy was in need of comfort, was licking him at intervals. 'Not even Superman could slice the mantle on thees one. He has been cut I am sure.'

To prove his point, he shinned up the wall like a monkey and began examining the top minutely. Even from a distance, the children could see his face change. He prized something from the wall. It glinted in the light. Putting it carefully in a side pocket of his cargo trousers he clambered back down. When he came over to them, he was almost shaking with rage.

'Is no accident. Is stupid meestake.' Opening his pocket, he withdrew a Stanley knife, a small, wickedly sharp blade often used by carpenters. 'Someone wedge this in joint of wall, maybe carpenters who come to fix it yesterday. Maybe they is talking too much – these workmen nowadays, they is not reliable – and forget it. Unfortunately, is in place where rope will be most – how you say – taut. When thees small boy Jimmy sit down in his harness, it cut and rope is snap.'

Rita and Bob tore in, hands flailing. They'd come directly from a ballroom dancing class and her sequinned gown and his velvet suit contrasted sharply with the general scruffiness of most of the climbers.

'Oh, my poor, sweet baby,' Rita cried, throwing her arms around Jimmy. 'I can't believe you're in one piece. And to think that we encouraged you to do this.'

She turned on Russ. 'What kind of cowboy outfit are you running here? My son could have broken his neck.'

Russ was mortified. 'Mrs Gannet, I must point out that we have impact matting beneath the wall so broken bones are extremely rare, but there is no doubt Jimmy has had a terrible fright. I can't apologise enough. I simply cannot explain how this happened. Ernesto, who checks our equipment, is meticulous. Safety is our watchword here. But it seems there might have been some oversight on the part of the company that built the wall. In thirty years as an instructor—'

'I'm afraid words are not going to be enough on this occasion,' interrupted Bob. 'We're talking a major lawsuit here. My boy might not have broken a bone, but there's stress . . . psychological trauma, perhaps years of counselling . . .'

'NO!'

Everyone turned in surprise. Jimmy's face was red with exertion and his hair was wilder than ever, but his eyes were bright with excitement. 'Nobody is going to be suing anybody, not today or ever. Mum, Dad, look at me. I'm happy. I climbed a cliff. I was a bit scared but I did it. For the first time in my life, I've had a proper adventure. And do you know what the best part was? My friends saved me.'

'It was nothing,' Laura said with a smile. 'If anything, you should thank Russ. His safety training was excellent. We'd rehearsed the drill and we knew what to do.'

'If the drill helped I'm grateful,' Russ said, 'but the truth is that your lightning response saved the day. All three of you showed courage and calmness in a crisis way beyond your years. There were many times on Everest when I could have done with friends like you.'

'Tariq and I just did what anyone would have done,' Laura said. 'It's Jimmy who's the brave one. Jimmy, when I'm a detective, you can be my sergeant any day.'

He flashed a grin. 'Umm, I'm going to be the great detective, remember, and you can be *my* sergeant!'

'All right, you two, stop with the rivalry,' teased Tariq. 'We've had enough excitement for one day.'

Bob and Rita stared at their son in astonishment. Minutes after a fall that could have been critical he was bantering with his new friends as if nothing had happened.

Laura decided to take advantage of their temporary silence to beat a hasty retreat. 'See you tomorrow, Jimmy. Come on, Skye, let's go for a walk.'

'See you,' said Tariq, shaking the boy's hand.

'See you,' Jimmy responded. 'Hey, Laura, don't forget about our plan.'

'I won't.'

'What was that all about?' Tariq asked when they were out in the corridor.

'A challenge.'

'A challenge?'

'Sort of a dare. Yes, I know, this morning I wanted to have as little as possible to do with him, but he suggested this game and, well, it sounded like fun. I said I'd talk it over with you. His idea is that we spend a day practicing being detectives.'

'How would that work?'

Laura's face lit up. She always leapt at any chance to talk about her detective hero. She immediately became so caught up in her story that she temporarily forgot about Jimmy's near death experience in the adventure centre.

'As you know, Detective Inspector Walker has had to spend a lot of time being someone he's not in order to crack a case. Once, he posed as a doddery old gardener at a castle; another time, he worked as a chef in a restaurant.

He's brilliant at it and he's very convincing. The villains rarely suspect a thing. Sometimes he'll pretend to be a random passerby at a murder scene, for example. He picks up all sorts of clues because people don't realise he's a policeman.'

Tariq grinned. 'And Jimmy thinks we should try the same thing on the ship where nobody knows us and we can be anyone we want?'

Laura looked at him. 'Yes. Do you think it's silly? I was worried that people might get upset if they find out we've lied to them, but Jimmy said that we could explain to them afterwards that we were only playing. On our last morning at sea or something. He dared us to do it for a day and whoever convinces the most people gets a free piece of chocolate cake.'

Tariq laughed. 'We'd get a free piece of chocolate cake anyway.'

'That's not the point. It's about the challenge – about seeing whether we could really convince people.'

They'd reached the door of their cabin.

'I'm game if you are,' Tariq said.

'Cool. Then let's do it.'

Laura opened the door and was relieved to see that Jimmy had not let himself in again. The cabin was peaceful. Through the French doors pillowy waves heaved and surged. A seabird swooped on an unseen fish. She hopped onto the bed and Skye snuggled up beside her.

'About what happened,' Tariq said. 'You were supposed to be the first climber, right? If Jimmy hadn't insisted on going up, it would have been you on the wall. You would have been the one to fall. The carpenter who left his Stanley knife in the joint, he could have put you in the hospital.'

Goosebumps rose on Laura's arms and she tugged the sleeves of her sweatshirt down. She'd talked animatedly about Jimmy's challenge on the way back from the adventure centre in the hope of distracting Tariq – and herself – from precisely that thought. There was a ninety-nine per cent likelihood that the knife had indeed been left behind by some inept, dangerously forgetful carpenter, as Ernesto had suggested. But there was no escaping the fact that it might also have been put there on purpose, perhaps even with the aim of hurting a specific person. After all, the rope was only severed because the knife was in the precise spot where it became taut. And Laura had been down in Russ's appointment book as the first climber of the day.

'You don't think . . . ?' Tariq picked at a thread on his jeans. He was reluctant to say the words out loud for fear of lending them power. 'You don't think it was . . . ?'

'Intended for me? No, of course not,' said Laura with a lot more confidence then she felt. 'Apart from Russ and Ernesto, how could anyone have known that I was due to climb first? It was coincidence.' She didn't want to say that, for days now, coincidences had been piling up to the point where it was starting to feel as if there was a lot more to them than chance. The last thing she wanted was to worry her best friend and spoil his special holiday.

'Come on,' she said, 'let's take Skye to cheer up my uncle.'

~ 11 ~

ON THEIR LAST morning at sea, they took Calvin Redfern a cup of coffee and a croissant and couldn't wake him. Usually he slept with one eye open but today he was dead to the world. After five minutes of trying to rouse him Laura was sufficiently concerned to consider defying her uncle's orders and call the ship's doctor.

She had the phone in her hand when he stirred and blinked sleepily at them. Seeing the time and their anxious faces, he said, 'Sorry if I've overslept, but it is your fault, you know. Laura, what were you doing creeping around my cabin in the middle of the night?'

She replaced the receiver. 'I wasn't.'

77

A small frown creased her uncle's brow but he was still smiling. 'Yes, you were. I heard you opening the bathroom cabinet. I spoke to you but you didn't answer and before I knew it I was asleep again. Were you checking up on me again?'

The uneasy feeling returned to Laura with full force. With a quick glance at Tariq, she said: 'Oh, I totally forgot. I had a headache and I came in to get some aspirin. In fact, I think I'll get another couple of tablets so if I need them another time I won't disturb you.'

She went to the bathroom cabinet and rattled the tub of aspirin. As far as she could tell nothing had been touched, but all her senses were on red alert. Her uncle had one of the sharpest minds she'd ever known. He was not in the habit of imagining midnight visitors. If he thought he'd heard someone in his cabin, he had. And what's more, he knew he had. Laura hadn't fooled him with her headache excuse.

Back in the cabin, her uncle had woken up sufficiently to read Tariq a few paragraphs from his Matt Walker book. They were both laughing. But it didn't last long. Before he'd even finished the page, Calvin Redfern's eyes were drooping.

He apologised again. 'I'm not sure why I'm so exhausted. Before I went to bed last night I was walking around my cabin and feeling so alert and ready to escape into the fresh air that I fully intended to surprise you by being dressed and ready for breakfast when you came in this morning. Now my head feels like cotton wool. Laura, would you mind making me an extra strong cup of coffee?'

It took Laura a couple of minutes to do as he asked, but by then her uncle was already snoring softly. No amount of shaking would wake him.

Tariq was amazed. 'I've never seen anyone doze off so quickly. He fell asleep in mid-sentence. I know his hard work back in Cornwall has worn him out, but over the past few days he's been like a caged lion, desperate to get out and start enjoying his holiday. He was laughing and joking. Now he's an invalid again. And what was all that about you being in his cabin in the middle of the night? I didn't hear you get up.'

Laura smoothed the covers over her uncle. 'I didn't. Maybe he dreamt it, but I don't think so. Tariq, something weird is going on with my uncle. I can't put a finger on what it is.'

Briefly, she told Tariq about her uncle's mysterious 3am meeting and about the hooks on the stairs that made her think of a tripwire. He immediately wanted to see them.

'They're here,' Laura said, leading him into the corridor and up to the second step. She stopped. 'At least they were.'

Not only had the hooks gone, there was nothing to indicate they'd ever been there. The paintwork was immaculate. There were a couple of specks of white on the steel of the stairs, but no way of telling how long they'd been there.

'I believe you,' Tariq said, seeing Laura's crestfallen face, 'especially since the light was broken at the time. Do you remember how it was working perfectly just a few minutes later? It's almost as if someone wanted it to fail so your uncle would fall. But who would do such a thing? It doesn't make any sense. Do you think your uncle suspected foul play?'

'Let's search his cabin while he's sleeping,' suggested Laura. 'There's bound to be a simple explanation for everything. Seriously, what are the chances of someone setting out to rob, harm or kill my uncle on a ship like the *Ocean Empress*?'

'Close to zero?'

'That's what I think. Besides, even if a thief did get into my uncle's cabin he or she wouldn't have found anything of value because Uncle Calvin's passport and money are in the safe in ours.'

'I'm sure you're right,' Tariq said. 'But let's search the cabin just in case.'

It was Tariq who found the pot of sleeping tablets on the bedside table. The reason Laura hadn't spotted it earlier was because the little brown container was identical to the one in which Calvin Redfern kept his pain medication. That bottle was on a shelf in the bathroom cabinet.

Laura studied the label, which was dated a year earlier and had her uncle's name on it. 'Now I'm confused. On the one hand, I'm relieved because it explains why he seems drugged. It's just that I can't imagine him making such a silly mistake. That makes me think there really was an intruder in his cabin last night and that that person swapped the bottles.'

Tariq looked over at Calvin Redfern, who was snoring softly. 'But why would anyone want to keep your uncle asleep? It doesn't make sense.'

'The only other explanation is that someone wants him out of the way. And why would they want that? *Who* would want that?'

'Maybe we should have Skye watch over your uncle,' Tariq suggested. 'Calvin Redfern will be glad of the company when he wakes anyway.'

They were on their way to fetch the husky when the ship's siren sounded and four breathless words burst from the tannoy: 'Pirates ahoy! Pirates ahoy!'

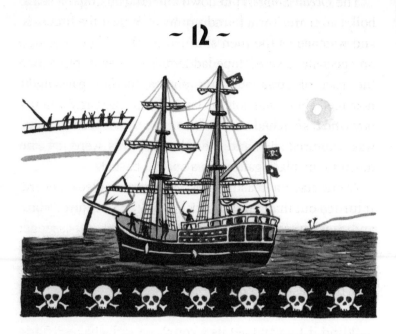

UP ON DECK every able-bodied passenger was hanging over the side, watching a black galleon approach. Its skull and crossbones flags billowed in the wind. Black-shirted pirates toiled on board and shinned up ropes and ladders.

'Is this a joke?' Tariq asked, unsure whether to laugh or be alarmed. 'Surely we're not about to be captured by modern-day pirates?'

'Well, there are modern-day pirates in Somalia and places like Indonesia who kidnap people all the time,' Laura told him. 'But from what my uncle says, they wear ordinary clothes and go about in small boats. I think these are actors.'

The *Ocean Empress* put down anchor, causing the sea to boil. Laura and Tariq found a quiet area near the lifeboats, and watched as the men shinned up the side of the ship on specially lowered rope ladders. They began playacting the part of swashbuckling pirates, taking passengers hostage. There was lots of laughter, particularly when a boy who'd snatched a cutlass from an unsuspecting pirate was 'captured'. He and the other captives were lowered down to the black galleon in a special basket.

At one stage, a treasure chest was manhandled on board. It turned out that it was a trick chest, like a conjurer's box, and there were gasps of amazement when a passenger who volunteered to climb into it vanished for several minutes. The pirate magician demonstrated for all to see that the chest was empty. But when he shut the lid and then reopened it, there she was, as large as life.

'Mind if I go and get us a couple of milkshakes?' Tariq wanted to know.

'Ooh, great idea. I'll have a strawberry one, please.'

Laura had been alone for barely a minute when a voice behind her growled: 'Ah, a lone captive!' She turned to see a gnarled pirate with a fake moustache and a permanent sneer, who also happened to be one of the tallest men she'd ever seen in her life. Close on his heels was a small, gangly man with an eye-patch and greasy black ringlets. He was gripping the handle of a large laundry hamper on wheels.

'Ever been curious to see a pirate's lair?' the tall man asked, flashing a gold tooth.

'No,' said Laura, 'I haven't. And I'm not interested in

being captured. I'm only standing here while I wait for my friend.'

The pirate chuckled. 'I've got news for you. Captives don't usually have a choice, do they, Lukas?' He took a step towards her.

There was something in his manner – a nervous aggression – that made Laura's heart start to pound. If this part of a game, then the game had gone too far.

'I'm curious,' she said, playing for time. 'Why do so many pirates wear eye-patches? Do you deliberately gouge out each other's eyeballs or are you just really bad sword fighters?'

'Hear that, Lukas? We got ourselves a feisty one. Well, well, well. I suppose I shouldn't be surprised. Last chance, young lady. Are you going to come with us willingly?'

Before Laura could move or respond, he'd lunged for her. Grabbing both her wrists in one enormous hand, he covered her mouth with the other – a hairy mitt reeking of fish. As Laura fought and kicked for all she was worth, Lukas dragged the laundry hamper closer.

Next thing she knew she'd been abruptly dropped on the deck and Lukas and the tall pirate were staggering around wiping strawberry milkshake from their eyes.

Tariq, who'd thrown it, helped Laura up and shielded her from the men.

'What's going on here?' demanded Fernando, appearing out of nowhere with Skye. The husky bounded over to Laura and she threw her arms around him. Never had she been so overjoyed to see him.

'Aww, tere's nutting goin' on,' whined Lukas, still

blinking away milkshake. His eyelashes and brows were thick with it. 'We were having a bit o' fun, tat's all.'

'It wasn't nothing,' Laura said furiously. 'They were trying to stuff me into that basket.'

Fernando glared at them. 'Is that true?'

''Course not, what do you take us for?' The tall pirate's lip curled and his gold tooth winked in the sun. 'You know as well as I do that we're not real pirates. We're a tourist attraction sent to welcome people to the Caribbean and make them laugh. I thought the young lady might like to see a trick we do with the basket, but she suddenly got scared. I was trying to comfort her.'

'By covering my mouth with your stinking hand? It's hard to laugh when you're being smothered.'

'I think you'd better return to your galleon before I call security or the young lady accidentally lets go of her dog,' Fernando said. 'I've heard that huskies are quite partial to pirates – even if they're only fake ones.'

'All right, all right. We're on our way. You'll get no trouble from us.'

'We was playing,' Lukas insisted. 'We didn't mean nutting by it.'

They departed with scowls and their basket.

'They weren't playing and they did mean something by it,' Laura said. 'Thank you all for saving me. Tariq, if you hadn't thrown your milkshake at them, something terrible would have happened.'

A shimmer caught her eye. It was a pale green badge with a picture of a smiling dolphin on the front above a banner on which MARINE CONCERN was written in a cheerful script. She slipped it into her pocket. Funny, the pirates hadn't struck her as the type who'd be overly worried about the conservation of sea creatures.

Fernando was agitated. 'Should I report this incident to security?'

As he spoke, they felt the deck vibrate. The *Ocean Empress* was on her way once more. The black galleon receded into the distance. Turquoise waters surrounded them and on the horizon was a hint of white sand and palm trees.

'Don't worry about it,' Laura said. 'I'm sure they were only acting. They just took it a bit far. As Matron would say: "All's well that ends well."'

~ 13 ~

'**PLEASE TELL ME** I'm dreaming,' Laura said. 'Or if I'm awake, tell me that I've had a brainstorm and forgotten the number of my uncle's cabin. It's not 135 after all but 133 next door, or it's not Deck C but Deck B.'

She stood at the door of the cabin where, barely an hour earlier, they'd talked to Calvin Redfern. It was empty. Not only was her sleeping uncle gone, together with his suitcase, toothbrush, books and medicine, but the place was spotless. The bed was made up with crisply ironed sheets, and the bathroom had fresh towels and a new bar of soap in it. The cabin smelled of mint and lemon.

Tariq shook his head in stunned disbelief. 'Let's not panic. There has to be an explanation.'

Laura clutched Skye for support. 'Like there was an explanation for my uncle's fall, or the hooks in the stairwell, or the Stanley knife hidden in the wall, or the mixed up sleeping tablets, or the 3am visitor back in St Ives?'

'Maybe he felt better and decided to get up and get organised so that he's ready when we reach Antigua at sundown,' suggested Tariq. 'The cleaners haven't been able to get in here all week so they probably swooped in and scrubbed the place. I bet you anything he's eating brunch in one of the restaurants. We could go up and join him.'

It all seemed so simple and so logical that a tide of relief washed over Laura. 'Oh Tariq, of course that's what's happened. He'll be in the Manhattan Grill, eating pancakes. You know how he loves them. Besides, we're on a ship in the middle of the ocean. How far can he have gone?'

But Calvin Redfern was not in the Manhattan Grill. Nor was he in the Happy Clam or the Blue Flamingo or in the gym, the spa or the pool. He wasn't ice skating, rock climbing, taking guitar lessons, or browsing for a new book in the gift shop.

'We're going to have to tell security,' Laura said, when they were forced to stop for food at around two. The exertion of searching the ship, plus a mounting feeling of panic, had left her feeling lightheaded. Tariq had a bad headache. Neither of them had eaten since the previous night. They'd been planning to have breakfast as soon as they'd taken Calvin Redfern his. The pirate visit had put a stop to that. And the drinks Tariq had fetched earlier had been splattered all over the men.

Tariq took a swallow of chocolate milkshake. 'That could be risky. What if they start asking questions about Skye or me? They might want to know why I don't have a boarding pass.'

'Well, technically we've not got permission to have Skye on the ship, but at least Rowenna emailed through his pet passport so he's legally allowed to be in the Caribbean. Still, we can lock him in our cabin just in case. As for you, there shouldn't be a problem. As my uncle said, they charge per cabin, not per person, and I have a ticket.'

Tariq finished his milkshake and pushed his plate away. 'This is such a weird situation. Where could your uncle possibly have gone?'

'I don't know,' Laura said. 'But I intend to find out.'

'We could ask Jimmy to help us hunt for him,' Tariq suggested. 'Even you admitted he has the makings of quite a good detective.'

'I did say that, but –'

'He won the dare fair and square.'

'He did, but that was mainly because there were so many . . . incidents . . . during the day. I was afraid he was going to injure himself or someone else. Besides we'll be arriving in Antigua in a few hours and he'll be helping Bob and Rita pack or explaining to various passengers that he isn't psychic or an archery prodigy but just plain old Jimmy Gannet. Look, my uncle can't possibly be missing. We're out on the ocean. He'll be somewhere obvious that we haven't thought to look. Come on, let's comb every deck again.'

The security manager was a scrawny man so white he could have been sculpted from feta cheese. Fittingly, his name was Viktor Bland. As he talked, his bony fingers incessantly rearranged the few strands of black hair still remaining on his head.

He was eating a steak and kidney pie when Laura and Tariq came rushing in to report Calvin Redfern's disappearance. Initially, he dismissed them out of hand, saying that if they made the smallest effort to search for him, they'd find him. When Laura explained that they'd searched for him for over two hours without success, he rolled his eyes.

He pulled a pad towards him with one corpse-like hand. The other scooped up another fork full of pie. 'Name?' he barked.

'Laura Marlin.'

'Your uncle's name is Laura?'

Laura rolled her eyes in return. 'No, that's *my* name. My uncle's name is Calvin Redfern.'

Viktor Bland stuffed the pie into his mouth and spluttered something indecipherable, spraying crumbs.

Laura leaned forward, thinking unkind thoughts about the man. 'Excuse me?'

Viktor switched on a desk microphone. 'Would passenger Calvin Redfern please come to the security office on Deck A. Your niece and her' – he glowered at Tariq – 'friend are waiting for you.'

He clicked off the microphone. 'Happy now? Can I finish my lunch?'

Laura felt foolish for not thinking of the tannoy system sooner. It would have saved them hours. Any minute now her uncle would walk through the door, ruffle her hair and give her one of his slow, kind smiles. He'd say, 'But I was sitting in the coffee shop all along. Didn't you see me? I was at that back table tucked behind the bar.'

They'd work out that whenever they were up on deck, searching for him, he was down below searching for them and vice versa. They'd all laugh about it.

But Calvin Redfern didn't show up. After forty uncomfortable minutes had passed, with Laura's accusing gaze growing colder by the second, the security manager grudgingly agreed to have a couple of his guards search the ship.

'If you are wasting my time now, in our busiest period, two hours before we dock in Antigua, I will not be answerable for the consequences,' he ranted at Laura. 'Your uncle might have to pay a large fine.'

'A man has gone missing on a ship which you're supposed to be keeping safe, and all you can think about is money,' she said angrily. 'You should be ashamed.'

He glared at her and issued veiled threats, but after that

he took his job more seriously. Not that it helped. Calvin Redfern could not be found.

Laura began to feel hysterical. 'This is insane. We're on a cruise ship full of people enjoying themselves. How could this happen? Oh, it's all my fault for leaving him alone.'

Tariq couldn't bear to see her so upset. 'Let's search his cabin again. Maybe we've missed something.'

'But we've already searched it three times.'

'Matt Walker would do it again.'

She gave a weak smile. 'Yes, he would.'

Perhaps because the cabin had been closed up for an hour or so, or perhaps because they were so determined to notice every detail, they immediately detected a change in the smell of the cabin. Along with the mint and lemon was a distinct smell of chocolate peanuts.

Laura's blood ran cold. She remembered the day at the adventure centre and that innocent smell took on a new and potentially terrible meaning.

With renewed urgency they did what detectives call a 'fingertip' search, going over the cabin centimeter by centimeter on their hands and knees.

It was Laura who found the playing card. It was wedged between the bed and the wall, which was why they hadn't seen it before and why even the cleaners had missed it. It fell out when Laura tugged back the mattress. She picked it up, took one look at the malevolent Joker on the front and burst into tears.

'They've got him, Tariq. The Straight A gang have got him.'

~ 14 ~

'*KIDNAPPED?* BY AN INTERNATIONAL criminal gang?' Viktor Bland wanted to throw his head back and laugh, but a crowd was gathering, sensing a drama. 'That's the most preposterous suggestion I've ever heard. Not on the *Ocean Empress* and not on my watch. It may have escaped your notice, dear girl, but we're in the middle of the ocean. Criminal gangs can't exactly roar in, guns blazing, and snatch our passengers.'

He said this last bit for effect and smiled at his audience, like an actor waiting for applause.

Laura gave him a freezing stare. 'It was the pirates who kidnapped him, I know it was.'

93

'The pirates? Oh, you mean, the actors sent by the Tourist Board to welcome you to the Caribbean? They've been coming aboard the *Ocean Empress* for eight years now and we've never had a complaint. They're a passenger favourite.'

'If that's the Caribbean's idea of a welcome, I'd rather take my chances with the sharks,' Laura retorted. 'Two of them tried to stuff me into a laundry hamper.'

Viktor Bland noted with relief that the ship was approaching the harbour. With any luck he could soon hand the problem of Laura and her missing uncle over to the Antiguan authorities. No doubt the man had had too much sun or too many cocktails and fallen asleep in a cupboard or under the bar. It had happened before.

'Are you listening?' demanded Laura.

In his whole career, Viktor had never met such an aggravatingly persistent girl. The serious, silent Bengali boy who accompanied her was even worse. He had clear, tiger's eyes that saw everything and missed nothing. It was very disconcerting.

'Miss Marlin, I appreciate that you're distressed and admittedly it's perplexing that your uncle has not yet come to light, especially since we're coming into port. But unless he's fallen overboard, or indeed jumped, and I can assure you we have people who watch very carefully for that sort of thing . . .'

'Laura! Tariq!' cried Rita Gannet, tottering over on high heels with Bob in her wake. 'There you are! We've been looking everywhere for you. We've been on the top deck watching Antigua grow bigger and bigger. What a sight it

94

is! Sand as white as snow and palms waving in the breeze.'

'Now is not the best time, Mr and Mrs Gannet,' said Tariq, attempting to steer the couple away. 'We're dealing with a crisis.'

'Laura! Tariq! What's going on? I've just heard that your uncle's gone missing.' Jimmy came running up, flushed with effort. His T-shirt looked as if it had had a fight with a cheeseburger and lost, and there were wisps of candyfloss in his hair. 'Where is he? What can I do to help?'

'I'M TELLING YOU FOR THE TENTH TIME, MY UNCLE HAS BEEN KIDNAPPED BY PIRATES,' Laura shouted at Viktor Bland.

'Kidnapped!' echoed a burly woman in a pink stetson, and the cry went out across the ship like an echo chamber:

'By *pirates*?' Jimmy said in awe.

'You mean, those phonies we saw earlier? What's the world coming to?' demanded a woman with a skunk-inspired hairstyle.

'KIDNAPPED! Who's been kidnapped?'

'I heard it was her uncle,' said the cowgirl.

'What's this about Laura and Tariq's uncle going missing?' demanded a woman with a turkey neck, bent under the weight of her gold jewellery. 'That's all they need. They're adopted, poor loves. Heartbreaking past they had in the Chillwood Institution for Unwanted Children. Before they were rescued by Calvin Redfern, a handsome fisheries investigator, they ate squirrels to survive.'

'Hang on a minute. They told us they were child geniuses who'd won a trip to the Caribbean in a Mensa quiz,' protested a man in a safari suit, who resembled a mad butterfly collector.

'And I believed them when they said they were junior athletes on their way to the Antiguan long jump championships,' a teenage girl put in bitterly.

'Laura! Tariq! What is the meaning of this?' roared Bob Gannet. 'Is this true? Have you told lies to everyone on the ship?'

'A very good question, sir,' said Viktor Bland, furiously rearranging his hair across his baldpate. He turned on the children. 'Is this whole story about a missing uncle nothing more than a fairytale concocted between you?'

'NO!' they shouted together.

'Laura and Tariq never lie,' said Jimmy, bravely positioning himself between his friends and their accusers. 'This whole situation is my fault. I asked them to play a game where we all pretended to be someone we're not. We wanted to practise being undercover detectives. We were planning to tell everyone the truth, but then this happened.'

'Please believe us,' Laura said desperately. 'My uncle has been snatched by the Straight A gang, one of the deadliest crime syndicates on earth. My guess is they shoved him in that Treasure Chest with the false back. They do that sort of thing all the time. Once they used a pizza boy disguise to kidnap . . . Oh, it's a long story. We'll explain later, but right now we need to call the police and find my uncle. Every second counts.'

'There is a simple way to solve this,' the butterfly man said silkily, 'and that's to answer one simple question.

Has anyone seen this elusive uncle? If they have, then he exists. If nobody has caught so much of a glimpse of him then it seems to me we must assume that he doesn't.'

'That's not fair,' protested Laura. 'Minutes after he boarded the *Ocean Empress*, he fell down some stairs and sprained both ankles and he's been confined to the cabin ever since. Nobody has seen him except Tariq and I. Oh, and the room service waiter.'

'Which room service waiter?' asked the woman in the Stetson. 'Luigi? Andre?'

'I don't know,' confessed Laura. 'We never saw him or her.'

'I'm the ship doctor,' said a silver-haired man stepping forward, 'and this is the first I've heard of a passenger with two sprained ankles.'

'What about you, Jimmy?' demanded Bob. 'You've seen a lot of Tariq and Laura this week. Have you seen the famous uncle?'

Jimmy went red to the roots of his wild hair. 'No, I haven't, but that doesn't mean anything. I believe them. They're my friends.'

'Not even their closest friend has laid eyes on this mythical uncle,' crowed Viktor Bland. 'It's all lies. One lie after another. They're stowaways plain and simple.'

'Oh, my goodness,' sighed Rita.

Overhead the sky glowed pink with the setting sun. The ship had shuddered to a stop. Streams of passengers were pouring out onto the harbour and Laura could feel the humid warmth of Antigua rising up to envelop her.

A voice she didn't recognise said: 'The police? We'll

happily call the police. They love it when we hand over stowaways.'

She turned to see the captain towering over them in immaculate whites. Two beefy guards flanked him, their biceps straining at their shirtsleeves.

Tariq murmured in Laura's ear: 'This could be bad.'

The woman in the stetson repeated: '*Stowaways?* On the *Ocean Empress?*'

'In this day and age?' The skunk woman was scandalised.

'I'm afraid so, ma'am,' said the captain. 'You see, we've searched our passenger list extensively. Not only can we can find no record of a Calvin Redfern on the ship, there is not one word about a Tariq Miah or a Laura Marlin either. As far as the *Ocean Empress* is concerned, you don't exist.'

'But that's impossible!' cried Laura. 'I won a competition. We have proof.'

The crowd began to buzz like angry bees.

'By some cunning method, you've taken advantage of our ship's hospitality for many days by stowing away in an empty cabin,' the captain went on. 'What's worse, I hear that you had yet another partner in crime. Fernando, bring out the evidence!'

'Aye, aye, Captain,' said Fernando, emerging from the throng with Skye.

Tariq rushed to take the husky from him, giving the waiter an apologetic look as he did so. 'Thank you for your help with Skye and for rescuing Laura from the pirates. We're very grateful to you.'

'It's not gratitude we want,' the captain cut in sourly.

'It's the many thousands of dollars you owe us for your berth on this ship.'

'It's true that we've made up a few stories and had a bit of fun during the week,' Laura said, 'but I'm begging you to believe us now. My uncle and I won the cruise in a raffle. Your records must show that somewhere. How else would we have got boarding passes?'

'What raffle?' demanded the captain. 'Where was this?'

'In St Ives, Cornwall, where we're from. A woman from a company called Fantasy Holidays sold me the winning ticket for a pound.' Even as Laura said it, she was aware of how far-fetched it sounded.

'You thought a one pound ticket entitled you to a luxury holiday for four, including your dog.'

Everyone laughed except Laura and Tariq.

'I know nothing about any competition or raffle,' boomed the captain. 'Nothing of that kind happens without my authority.'

Tariq said: 'If you allow us to return to our cabin, we can prove it, sir. A chauffeur in a limousine brought Laura a letter telling her she'd won. In the safe, we have tickets and vouchers and everything.'

The captain drew himself up to his full height, which was considerable. 'A short time ago, I authorised the steward to open the safe in cabin 126. There was nothing in it. No passports and certainly no tickets or boarding passes. Now I think we've heard quite enough lies for one day. Viktor, call the police.'

'Quite right,' agreed the security manager, finding his tongue. 'I can't believe I was taken in by the story of the vanished uncle. Angus and Dreyton, detain these children for further questioning. We'll hand them to the authorities when we dock.'

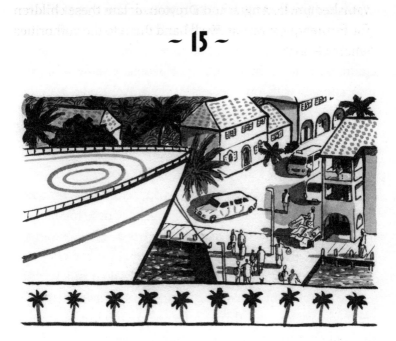

15

THE THING THAT Laura wanted most was for Tariq to shake her awake and tell it had all been some awful nightmare. That she'd fallen asleep on the sofa at number 28 Ocean View Terrace in St Ives. That there'd never been a competition involving a holiday in the Caribbean and that she'd never won it. That Calvin Redfern was safe, and that Rowenna would be making them a cottage pie for dinner.

Unfortunately, this particular nightmare was real. Angus and Dreyton moved to grab them, but halted when Skye gave a blood-curdling growl. Tariq held tight to the husky's collar. He gave the sailors a cool look, as if to say, 'Come any closer and I'll let go.'

All at once there was a commotion. The crowd parted like the Red Sea and through it came a couple dressed from head to toe in white. It was the kind of floaty cloud white worn by the types of people who never come into contact with dirt because they travel exclusively by limousine and jet and have mansions staffed by fleets of cleaners. They had matching tans, gold jewellery and celebrity sunglasses. The woman had a mane of cascading blonde hair.

'My angels, how I've missed you,' cried the woman, holding out her arms to Laura and Tariq. 'Come to Mama.'

There was a collective gasp from the gathered passengers. Laura and Tariq were stunned.

'Who the heck are you?' Viktor Bland asked rudely.

The man in white gave no indication he'd heard him. He stepped forward and thrust a brown, manicured hand in the captain's direction. 'My dear sir, forgive us for boarding your magnificent ship in such an undignified fashion, but it came to our attention that our beloved adopted children have been the cause of a small riot. Sebastian LeFever at your service. And this is my wife, Celia. I believe you've met Laura and Tariq.'

Laura's blood ran cold. She suddenly realised what was happening and she saw from Tariq's face that he did too. The Straight A gang must have bugged their cabin and/or Laura's beach bag. They'd overheard the stories the children had invented and the unfolding crisis over Laura's apparently non-existent uncle, and decided to use it as a ploy to kidnap the pair in full view of everyone.

The crowd began to buzz again.

'The children of gazillionaires. Fancy them stowing away like common criminals! What a scandal.'

The captain turned red and began to bluster: 'I'm so sorry, Mr LeFever. There seems to have been a misunderstanding. We thought . . . well, you see, we couldn't find a record . . . And the girl kept talking about a kidnapped uncle.'

Sebastian LeFever slapped him heartily on the back. 'Say no more about it, my good man. We often book the children's travel arrangements under assumed names for their own protection – to foil those who would hold them for ransom, you understand. If you check your passenger list for a couple of cabins held in the name of Fantasy Holidays Limited, I think you'll find that all is in order. It was a bit naughty of the children to bring their dog, but you're most welcome to invoice me at Clear Moon Estate if there's any extra charge. Now if you'll excuse us, we must say hello to our son and daughter. We've missed them terribly.'

'Of c-c-course,' stuttered the captain. 'And on behalf of Heavenly Cruises, may I again express our sincerest apologies . . .'

Sebastian, who smelled of starch and expensive cologne, bent down and hugged Laura stiffly. Celia embraced her with an ecstatic fervour, crumpling her white linen dress.

Sebastian marched up to Tariq and held out his hand. 'Son, how you've grown.'

'Thank you, Sir,' Tariq said politely. 'It's very nice to see you and Mother.'

'But who is the uncle they were panicking about?'

persisted Rita. 'They seemed sincerely distressed about him.'

Celia LeFever's ice-blue eyes alighted on Mrs Gannet with the same expression with which she might have regarded a fly in her soup. 'A much-loved bodyguard,' she explained. 'Regrettably, Mr Redfern was called away on urgent business and had to disembark the ship without delay and without saying goodbye to the children. Not to worry, they'll be seeing him soon enough.'

She smiled at Laura with all the warmth of a melting glacier. 'You'd like that, wouldn't you, darling?'

'I certainly would,' said Laura, giving her a look that would have reduced a lesser woman to a pile of smouldering ashes.

As Celia turned away, Tariq murmured in Laura's ear: 'Is this what people mean when they talk about being caught between the devil and the deep blue sea? Either we're arrested for being stowaways or we allow ourselves to be kidnapped by gangsters.'

'Those seem to be our options,' Laura whispered back. 'You know you're in trouble when the Straight A's seem like your best bet.'

Jimmy Gannet emerged panting and dishevelled from the dispersing, gossiping crowd. He had the look of a puppy that had been kicked, but it was obvious he was doing his best to ignore what he'd seen and heard and keep faith in his newfound friends.

'It's not true, is it?' he said, his small, bright brown eyes searching theirs. 'Tell me it isn't true.'

'Ready, kids?' Sebastian barked. 'Your mother and I have dinner reservations.'

Surreptitiously, Laura reached into her pocket and removed the badge she'd found on the deck after the pirates had left. She had no idea whether or not the men had dropped it, and if they had, whether it was remotely significant. But right now she was prepared to clutch at any available straw.

She reached out and took one of Jimmy's hands in hers, pressing the badge into it. 'I'm sorry, Jimmy. We didn't mean to lead you on, really we didn't. It was a game that went too far. I hope you'll forgive us in time. I would like to say something that is one hundred per cent true. If you keep dreaming and practicing, you'll grow up to be better than Matt Walker. My advice to you would be to start immediately.'

'Ready?' said Sebastian impatiently.

Laura smiled. 'We're ready.'

16

'**YOU'RE IN OUR** hands now and we're going to make you pay.'

Celia LeFever almost hissed the words into Laura's ear as they walked along the jetty in the dusk to a waiting stretch limousine.

'I'm sure you will,' Laura said though gritted teeth while pretending to smile at passing passengers. 'The way we'll make you pay if you've harmed my uncle.'

She kept close to Tariq and Skye, watching for the smallest chance of escape. It was hard to believe that only a few hours ago she'd woken in her bunk on the *Ocean Empress* practically bursting with excitement at the prospect of seeing Antigua – the island paradise with three hundred and sixty-five beaches. Now she was here and it felt like a nightmare.

The end of the jetty thronged with T-shirt sellers and plump, gaily-dressed Caribbean women sitting on rainbow-bright sarongs spread with homemade jewellery. An artist appealed to tourists to buy his paintings. 'Have pity on a starving painter; I need money for my dinner.' A shrivelled old man with sad eyes drank tea from a glass mug in front of a pink-painted café as the last sliver of sun melted into the sea.

As they approached the limousine, the shop lights flickered on. The sky had turned violet. Night was falling over Antigua.

Sebastian and two bodyguards in black suits brought up the rear. Laura was shocked to see that the chauffeur was the same smartly dressed young man who'd handed her balloons and complimented Mrs Crabtree back in St Ives. The only difference was that he was now wearing one dangling earring made from a silver chain, a pearl and a couple of guineafowl feathers.

Skye growled at him. It was obvious he remembered him.

'So you knew all along?' Laura said in disbelief as she was shepherded into the limo by the thuggish bodyguards. 'You actually stood there congratulating me when you knew all the time it was a trap?'

He shrugged and gave her the same cocky grin. 'Only doing my job, Miss Marlin. Only doing my job. I admit I was taken aback when I found you were only a kid, but, hey, I just does the work and takes the money.'

He snapped to attention as Sebastian came round to check what was taking so long. 'Everything going to plan?' the man in white asked abruptly.

The chauffeur saluted. 'Smooth as silk, Mr LeFever. Smooth as silk. Make yourself comfortable and I'll ride the tide home.'

Skye lay on the floor of the limo between Laura and Tariq, regarding the LeFevers and bodyguards with hostile blue eyes. The children were poised to jump or run if the slightest opportunity presented itself, but that was as likely as Christmas in January. The limo doors were locked and the glass was, Celia informed them, bulletproof.

'Just in case you get any ideas.'

As far as Laura could tell, it was not ideas that were required. It was the strength and speed of ten Olympians. One of the bodyguards was built like a wrestler and the other looked like a marathon runner. They had all bases covered. The children had already nicknamed them Little and Large.

Laura felt sick. This was all her fault. If she'd listened to her uncle and realised that winning a Caribbean Holiday for a pound was too good to be true – that there had to be a catch – they wouldn't be in this position. Calvin Redfern would not be in mortal danger, and she, Skye and Tariq would not have been kidnapped.

The terrifying part was that it had all been so carefully calculated. Every detail had been worked out. Fantasy Holidays Ltd had always intended the winning raffle ticket to go to Laura or Calvin Redfern. The separate cabins, the tripwire that had felled her uncle, even the disappearance of their passports – everything had been planned. Their passports, including Skye's pet papers, had magically reappeared as the LeFevers escorted them through customs before being spirited away as they exited. Their kidnappers' presence at passport control had seemed most unorthodox, but from what Laura could make out they'd managed to forge documents identifying themselves as the children's legal guardians.

Laura had considered making a scene in the customs hall until the police came to their rescue, but the bodyguards had taken Skye through separately. Sebastian had warned her that if she put a foot wrong she'd never see her husky again.

Outside the dark limo windows, pinpricks of light showed through the waving palm trees. Laughing boys roasted corn on a roadside barbecue, red sparks flying. Goats ambled leisurely across the road. Whole families sat on the porches of crumbling clapboard houses with plates on their laps, candles making tigerish shapes of their faces. Night creatures sang and croaked.

Celia and Sebastian sat in the rear of the limo and talked in low voices, glancing at the children from time to time. The bodyguards sat on either side of Laura and Tariq in the seat behind the driver, watching their charges with diminishing interest. It was clear that they thought two eleven-year-olds presented a minimal threat. Skye was a different matter. Large had threatened to push him out of the door at high speed if he so much as whimpered.

'He's a three-legged dog,' Laura said. 'What kind of monster are you?'

'A monster from your worst nightmares,' he leered.

'Skye,' called Laura softly, and the husky was on the seat in a bound. He sat squeezed between her and Tariq, facing the road ahead, tongue lolling.

'If that mutt damages the limo, we'll send him to the fur factory,' Sebastian warned. 'He'll make a great coat.'

'Why are you doing this?' Laura demanded. 'What is this about? Where are you taking us? Are you taking us to my uncle?'

Sebastian bared small white teeth. 'So many questions, Miss Marlin. Don't you worry your pretty little head. All will become clear in good time.'

'I hope you understand the risk you're taking,' Tariq said. 'Calvin Redfern will never let you get away with this.'

Sebastian laughed. 'It speaks! Well, son, let me be the first to inform you that the Straight A's have spent years perfecting the art of the kidnap. We most assuredly will get away with it. As for Calvin Redfern, he doesn't exactly have a choice.'

Laura's eyes roamed the limo, searching for an escape route. Tucked into the side panel of the left door was an orange cylinder. She was fairly confident that it was a signal launcher – a device used by sailors to set off emergency flares. A sort of mini rocket launcher. Her uncle had shown her one on a boat in St Ives. It was an odd thing to have in a limo and suggested that the LeFevers spent time at sea in situations that had the potential to become emergencies. She wondered what those situations were.

She did a mental rehearsal of snatching it from the side pocket, aiming it at the seat or the carpet and pulling its cord or trigger. Theoretically it would cause a fire, creating a diversion that might allow them to escape. But if it went wrong . . . Laura imagined blinding or burning someone in the car, perhaps even Tariq. It was not worth it. She'd have to wait for another opportunity and hope that it didn't come too late.

The glass panel that separated driver from passengers slid back and the chauffeur enquired: 'Everything all right wit' you, folks?'

Laura felt like screaming, 'You've kidnapped three people and a dog after dragging them halfway across the world on an elaborate con, how can everything be all right?' but then she noticed something interesting. Skye was fixated on the chauffeur's earring. A hunting light had come into his blue eyes. Laura had seen it only a couple of times before, but it had sent a chill through her. She loved him with all her heart but she never forgot that the wildness of his wolf forebears still lived in him.

As subtly as she could, she reached across and squeezed Tariq's hand to alert him. He followed her gaze and tensed.

The chauffeur turned his head to check for traffic at an intersection and accelerated rapidly. His earring jerked and danced. As fast as a striking cobra, Skye had the earring between his jaws, almost pulling the chauffeur's earlobe off. The man let out a screech of fright and pain and lost control of the car. It mounted a boulder on the roadside, burst a tyre and rolled twice.

Laura and Tariq, who were strapped in, had a hazy awareness of crunching metal and breaking glass. The limousine filled with black smoke. Everybody shouted at once. Skye barked frantically. The chauffeur slammed on the brakes as the carpet caught fire.

'Get out! Get out!' yelled Sebastian, wrenching at the door handle. Laura and Tariq stumbled into the night, their lungs burning, bruised but alive. The thin bodyguard staggered bloodily from the car and lost consciousness. The other fell to his knees retching. The hem of Celia's dress had caught fire and Sebastian was beating it out with a palm frond. The chauffeur was slumped over the steering wheel, covered in broken glass. Once Celia was safe, Sebastian and Large dragged him free.

'Are you thinking what I'm thinking?' Tariq asked Laura between coughs.

Laura grabbed Skye's collar. 'Yes, but wait one second.' In the shadows near the car was Celia's bag, thrown there by Sebastian. Some of its contents had spilled. Laura grabbed a fistful of dollar notes and their passports. 'Is it still called stealing if you take stolen money from kidnappers?'

For an answer, Tariq grabbed her hand and they fled into the night. There were shouts, but before anyone could come after them the limousine exploded. The blast was so deafening that Laura's ears rang for several minutes afterwards. Shards of burning metal flew in all directions. A great ball of white flame ballooned into the sky. The air was hot enough to roast potatoes.

Laura and Tariq ran without looking back. Still coughing and wheezing from the smoke, they tore through the darkness with no aim except to put as much distance between them and their captors as possible. There was no moon. At times, they could barely see their hands in front of their faces.

Tariq stopped. His lungs were burning. 'Why don't we give Skye his head and see if his instincts take over? He might lead us to safety.'

Released from his lead, the husky didn't hesitate. He led them along a narrow path through a grove of ferns and trees, past the shell of a ruined house, and across a darkened building site. A stitch which started as a pinprick in Laura's side rapidly became a twisting knife. By the time they reached a dirt road, Tariq was limping and she was in agony. In front of them was a line of palm trees and a silvery swathe of beach. Fishing boats winked like diamonds on the sea beyond.

Laura collapsed on the overgrown verge. 'That's it,' she panted. 'I don't care if they catch us. I can't move another step.'

Tariq sank to the ground beside her. He lay back and shut his eyes. Only Skye was keen to keep running.

Through the darkness came the clip-clop of hooves. A horse and cart rattled round the bend and pulled up beside them. A white-haired Caribbean man with a hat full of holes and a jacket full of patches gazed down at them.

'Well, dis ain't some'at dat Jess and I see every night. Youse all look weary and a bit sorry for youselves and we don't tolerate no long faces here in da Caribbean. Can I offer you folks a ride?'

17

THE BLUE HAVEN Resort had three swimming pools, five restaurants, two tennis courts, two private beaches, a gymnasium, a spa and a small cinema. Guests stayed in white clapboard villas scattered across five acres of grounds, lush with emerald grass and tropical vegetation alive with geckos, frogs and iridescent green hummingbirds collecting nectar from pink honeysuckle blossoms. Scarlet and orange hibiscus waved at the entrance of each villa.

'Who'd have thought that the chauffeur who tricked me in St Ives a week or so ago would end up indirectly setting us free purely because he was vain enough to put on that ridiculous feather earring,' Laura remarked the following morning as she and Tariq sat on the balcony of Guava Villa tucking into a breakfast of fried plantains, baked beans, scrambled eggs and pancakes dripping with maple syrup. Skye crunched up bacon slices at their feet.

'I almost feel sorry for Celia and Sebastian LeFever,' Tariq said, spearing a piece of pancake and several slices of plantain. 'When Calvin Redfern escapes or we find him, which will happen, their lives won't be worth living.'

'You can't possibly feel sorry for them,' Laura told him. They'd enjoyed an early morning swim in the bay and her short blonde hair was standing up in spikes. 'I hate to imagine what grisly fate they had in store for us. They're the kind of people who keep sharks in their swimming pool. We'd have been fed to them, a limb at a time.'

Watching pelicans dive for fish in the lagoon below them, Laura almost pinched herself. It was hard to take in that they were temporarily safe and in this beautiful place when it had seemed certain their visit to Antigua would end in arrest or worse. Collapsed on the roadside the previous night, their situation and that of her uncle had seemed hopeless. Then, like Good Samaritans, Joshua and his old horse had come along.

'Where you folks headed?' he'd asked them, as if there was nothing in the least unusual about coming across an English girl, a Bengali boy and a Siberian Husky sitting on the roadside in the moonlight.

'Blue Haven Resort,' Tariq answered, quick as a flash. 'We're staying there. We took our dog for a walk and got a bit lost.'

'Dat right?' Joshua muttered but he didn't say anything.

'Well, hop in, boy. Don't know exackerly which hotel dat one is. I ain't from around here. But I'm guessing it's near Blue Haven bay, not ten minutes down dis here track.'

And with a click of Joshua's tongue and flick of the reins, they were on their way.

'Are you nuts?' Laura whispered to Tariq as they bumped through the darkness along a beach road. The air smelled of coconut and sea salt. Skye hung over the side of the cart, fur ruffling in the breeze, determined not to miss a single scent. 'The Straight A gang booked us in there. We might as well call them and say, "We're staying in the most obvious place in Antigua. Come and get us!"'

'It's because it's so obvious that we should go there,' Tariq told her. 'They won't think of looking for us there for days, and by then we'll be long gone. Anyway, grown-ups always underestimate kids. They don't think we can find our way out of a paper bag. Celia and Sebastian will be picturing us as couple of crying babies, lost in the rainforest, right now. The last thing that would occur to them is that we might hitch a ride to our hotel, calmly check in and stay the night.'

'If the hotel allow us to check in without a grown up,' Laura said. 'They might not. They might even call the police. But if it works, it's a great idea. Matt Walker says the simplest plan is usually the best one.'

She scooted along the wooden bench. 'You said you're not from around here, Joshua. Where's home?'

He pointed at the shimmering sea. 'Dat's home, right der.'

Laura thought at first that he meant he lived on a boat,

but then she saw it: a dark shape on the horizon. A swirl of cloud obscured the top.

'Dat der's Montserrat.'

'Montserrat, the volcano island?' Laura felt her heart clench. It had been the part of the trip her uncle had been most looking forward to.

'Sure is, honey love.' Only with Joshua's accent it sounded like 'onny lov'.

'Were you there when it erupted?' Tariq asked excitedly. He'd been learning about volcanoes at school and found them fascinating.

'Sure was. And for tree years before dat when earthquakes trembled and rocked da island like it was a dinosaur wit' indigestion. Da Soufriere Hills Volcano erupted on 18 Joolly 1995 after lying dormant for centuries. For two years dat volcano billowed smoke twenny-four seven. Burning rocks and steam came pouring down the mountain. Dey buried Plymouth, our capital city. Nowadays, it ain't nutting but a ghost town.'

'My uncle says that two-thirds of the islanders were forced to flee and that most of them never went back,' Laura said. 'Is that was happened to your family?'

At the mention of family she was reminded once again of her uncle's plight. Her stomach heaved. Where was he? Had they hurt him? Was he afraid? Would she ever see him again? She took a deep breath. Yes, she told herself firmly, she would. She definitely would.

The cart slowed. An arching blue sign announced the Blue Haven Resort. A security guard stepped from his hut and regarding them enquiringly. Joshua was talking but she'd missed some of it.'. . . because of dem skeletons,' he was saying.

'I beg your pardon,' Laura said. 'Would you mind repeating that?'

'I say my wife and I were 'vacuated after the volcano, but we went back soon as we could. We lost everything but we wanted to help rebuild our homeland. Dey call it da Emerald Isle, you know. Folks say it's as lush and green and beautiful as Ireland. All was coming along nicely till around one year ago when da skeletons started.'

Tariq craned forward. 'What skeletons?'

'Skeletons dat dance on the slopes of da volcano. I tell my wife it's a trick of da light, but she tell me she see dem clear as day close to the dolphin place. Other people see dem too. Not once. Two, three, five times. So I move her to Antigua because she weren't giving me no peace about it.'

'You said something about a dolphin place,' Laura reminded him. 'An aquarium or dolphinarium, you mean?'

'No, no, it's a scientific company. Researching how to save whales and sea life and such like. My friend, Rupert Long, he's a scientist his self – a volcanologist – he say dey all crazy nutters down dere. Da Government advised dem not build dat laboratory right next to da volcano, but dey insist it's important for der work.'

Why is it that people who are passionate about saving whales and other mammals are always labelled as 'crazy', Laura wondered.

The security guard strode up to them, bristling. 'Move it along,' he said sharply. 'No loitering. This is private property.'

'We're guests of the hotel,' Laura informed him. Skye loomed out of the darkness, snarling, and the guard jumped back.

She hugged the old man. 'Joshua, you've saved our lives. I don't know how to thank you.'

'Go to Montserrat,' he said, shaking Tariq's hand. 'We need tourists if we is ever to recover. If you need help or want to get up close and personal wit a volcano, find Rupert Long and tell him Joshua sent you. Take care y'all. Nice dog, by da way.'

With a click of his tongue and a squeak of wheels, he and his horse were gone.

'Now look here, kids,' said the guard, 'I don't know what you think you're playing at, but you're not staying at Blue Haven. The kind of people who come here arrive by limo or private taxi. They don't turn up on the back of a cart and they don't bring wolves.'

Laura thrust their passports into his hand, lifted her chin and stared at him with as much authority as she could manage. 'My name's Laura Marlin and this is Tariq Miah and my husky, Skye. Back in England we won a prize for a dream holiday, which has so far been a complete nightmare. The final straw was when our limousine burst into flames. We're hoping for more from your lovely resort. Now if you'll excuse us, we're very tired and we'd like to check in.'

The manager behind the reception desk hadn't been quite so easy to convince.

'Your name is on the booking so I don't have a problem with that,' she told Laura. 'But it's most unorthodox to have children checking in on their own, especially with no luggage. Tell me again how you came to arrive here without your uncle.'

Laura decided that if they were ever to get a meal, a shower and a decent night's sleep, now was the time to be economical with the truth. 'He's a detective,' she explained, omitting to mention that Calvin Redfern had left the police force over a year earlier and now investigated illegal fishing. 'He's tied up with an important case – a kidnapping case – and has been delayed, but he'll be with us as soon as he can. He apologises and asks for your cooperation and understanding at this difficult time.'

As she'd suspected, the word 'detective' had a magical effect. In a matter of minutes, she, Tariq and Skye were on a golf cart being whisked through the palms and vines to their villa. They'd fallen asleep to a soundtrack of cicadas and frogs and the soothing swish of the sea.

'The problem,' Laura said at lunchtime the next day, 'is that we don't know where to start looking. Antigua is a huge island. My uncle could be anywhere. We might as well search for a star in the sky or a grain of sand on one of the three hundred and sixty-five beaches.'

She rested her elbows on the railings of the Driftwood Kitchen, a thatched diner open to the elements, and gazed down at the lagoon. She felt very despondent. It was bizarre being in the island paradise she'd dreamt of, but being too frantic about the fate of her uncle to enjoy it.

On the white shore below her, families and bronzed young couples paddled in water dappled with every conceivable shade of blue. Teenagers made comical attempts to windsurf or lay sprawled on deck chairs, baking in the honeyed sunlight, oblivious to the darker side of the Caribbean.

'We will find him,' Tariq said determinedly. 'I don't care what it takes, we are going to do it.'

He perched restlessly on the stool beside Laura, absent-mindedly rubbing the husky's ears and scanning every face that passed. They both knew that it was only a matter of time before the Straight A gang figured out where they were. If you were eleven years old and a stranger to it, Antigua felt as big as Africa. If you were an adult with limitless money and knew the island like the back of your hand, it was child's play. And Celia and Sebastian could afford to hire every able-bodied man in Antigua to comb the island until they were found.

Tariq sipped the water from a hairy coconut. As they'd hoped, all meals and drinks were included in their prize, and Celia's money had paid for some extra essentials: clean T-shirts, shorts, trousers, socks, underwear, sunblock, toothpaste and toothbrushes, swimming costumes, sweatshirts and a backpack.

'Let's start with what we know,' Tariq said. 'Or with what we think happened. We're pretty sure that Calvin Redfern was kidnapped by a couple of Straight A gang members posing as pirates. If that's true, we could make enquiries about the pirate galleon and ask if there were any changes of staff that day.'

'That's a good idea in theory, but what if the pirates have friends on the boat or actually work on the boat themselves?' Laura said. 'We'd be walking right into the Straight A gang's hands.'

'Okay, how about doing the obvious thing again? We could go to the police.'

'And say what? That my uncle, who we have no proof was ever on the ship, has been kidnapped by the Straight A gang? Dozens of people saw the LeFevers claim us as their children on the ship, and heard us call them Mum and Dad. They're about as likely to believe that the LeFevers are part of an international crime syndicate as they are to believe that pirate actors put Calvin Redfern in a conjurer's trunk.'

She sighed. 'What we need is a clue. Just one tiny clue.'

A waitress with a gap-toothed smile and a name tag identifying her as Ira put two spicy shrimp salads, a bottle of Susie's hot sauce and a basket of bread on the narrow ledge that served as a table in the Driftwood Kitchen. 'Enjoy!'

'Thank you,' said Laura, forgetting her worries for a moment and smiling as Ira offered a large bone to Skye. He took it delicately and carried it over to a nearby patch of lawn. 'Skye says thank-you too. You've just made a husky very happy.'

'Happy is good. Happy is what we aim to do.' Ira brushed Laura's fair skin with her dark hand. 'Very sensible you are, darlin'. Staying out of the sun on the first day. A lotta our guests, they so excited to see our gorgeous clear water, they do nothing but swim and roast, swim and roast, like they hogs on a spit. By nightfall they're about ready to be carved. They has to spend the rest of their vacation in the shade, plastered with aloe vera.'

'Are there sharks in the bay?' Tariq asked her.

'Only on Sondays,' she retorted, straight-faced. Turning away she giggled, delighted at her own joke.

'Hey Laura, look at the back of her T-shirt,' Tariq said in a low voice. '"Marine Concern". Wasn't that the name on that badge you showed me on the ship, the one that had a smiling dolphin on it?'

He hopped up and went over to the counter, where the waitress was loading a tray with iced drinks. 'Excuse me, Miss Ira,' he said, 'I noticed the dolphin on your shirt. What is Marine Concern? Is it a charity?'

She beamed at him over the top of a tray of Pina Coladas. Polite children were a rarity at Blue Haven so she made a special effort when she came across them. 'You like dolphins and whales? Marine Concern, they doin' research on how best to save 'em. They very popular here in the islands. People give 'em millions to continue their studies.'

'Laura and I love dolphins and whales,' Tariq told her. 'Where is Marine Concern located? We'd really like to visit.'

Ira hoisted the tray onto her shoulder. 'You'll need a helicopter or a boat. And a life insurance policy. They is based in Monsterrat – right close to the volcano. They is either brave or crazy, that much I know. That volcano, it could go any day. Believe me when I tell you, you don't wanna go anywhere near it.'

He thanked her for her help and returned to Laura and his shrimp salad.

'Montserrat?' Laura said. 'You mean, the Emerald Isle with the dancing skeletons and the volcano that could erupt at any moment? Sounds like the kind of place I've been waiting to visit my whole life.'

Tariq couldn't help laughing. 'All I'm saying is it's the only clue we have. You thought there was a chance that the pirates might have dropped it. What if you're right? The pirates didn't strike me as the kind of people who care about dolphins.'

'Mmm, I doubt if those pirates care about their own mothers. And if Marine Concern is the place Joshua mentioned – the one with "crazy nutter" scientists working in the shadow of the volcano, it might be worth a visit. Where better to hide my uncle than a place where nobody wants to go because, any day now, a river of orange lava is going to come pouring down the mountain and swallow everything.'

Tariq sprinkled hot sauce all over his shrimp. His eyes met Laura's and she saw behind his smile a steely determination. 'How soon do we leave?' he said.

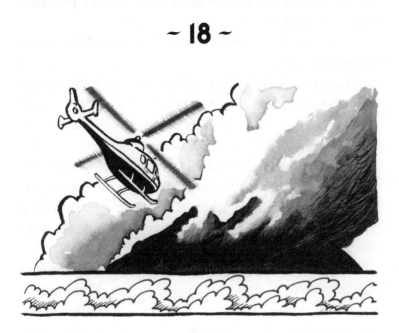

18

AT 4 P.M. THEY were at the helicopter pad for the last volcano tour of the day. Laura had been worried that without their competition vouchers – snatched by the Straight A gang – they wouldn't be able to afford the flight, but it turned out that Calvin Redfern had been so excited about seeing Montserrat, he'd reserved a couple of spots in advance before they'd even left Cornwall.

It was eerie to see her uncle's name on the register. It was almost as if he was speaking to her from . . . From where? Laura had no idea. 'Beyond the grave' was the phrase that popped into her head, but she pushed it out. Thinking positively had saved her life once before, and she was determined to use it to save her uncle's.

'Sorry kids, no pooches allowed,' the pilot told them when he arrived. A button nose and a cow's lick at the front of his fair hair gave him a cartoon character appearance. He barely looked old enough to drive, let alone fly a helicopter.

Laura had her response prepared. 'He's not a pooch, he's a police dog, and my uncle, Detective Inspector Redfern, urgently needs him to help solve a case in Montserrat. It's a matter of life and death.'

In a way, every word was true.

'A police dog you say. A matter of life and death. That puts a different slant on things.'

He gave them a sideways grin. 'You're not messing with me, are you?'

'We're not messing with you,' Tariq assured him. 'Skye is urgently needed to track down a missing person.'

'So urgently you thought you'd take a volcano tour first?'

'That,' Laura informed him, 'is for research purposes.'

He looked over at the hangar, which also served as an office. 'If my manager was here, he'd kill me for even considering it. Health and safety and all that.'

'He's not?' Laura asked hopefully.

The young man tugged at his cow's lick and scowled. 'He's on vacation again. Oh, what the heck. You're my last passengers of the day. If it's a matter of life and death . . .'

The volcano was smoking. That was a shock. So was the sight of the former capital city, its shops and houses crushed and upended, all coated in a thick blanket of greeny-grey volcanic ash.

'That's Plymouth,' explained the pilot. 'Forty feet of ash and mud poured over the place and crushed it as if it was a toy village. I always think it looks like the abandoned set of some science fiction disaster movie.'

To reach Montserrat they flew across an expanse of aquamarine sea so clear they saw a couple of feeding whales. From the air, Antigua really was a paradise. A tropical island fringed with exquisite beaches and inviting lagoons. Montserrat was small by comparison, but the part of the island undamaged by the volcano was the emerald green Joshua had talked about. Pastel-painted houses dotted the third of the island deemed safe from the lava flows. Cows and goats grazed on the edges of patchwork fields.

The helicopter doors were glass from floor to ceiling and the craft tipped and rolled as the pilot pointed out the sights. It was like being whooshed across the sky in a glass bubble. As they buzzed around the volcano's grey rim, Laura had to fight back a feeling of vertigo.

The closer they drew to the crater, the more ominous it looked. A column of smoke plumed into the late afternoon sky. At its centre was an orange glow, though whether that was the volcano's molten heart or the setting sun Laura found difficult to tell. She had a flashback to her nightmare in St Ives – the one in which the Fantasy Holidays travel woman had dangled her over a molten pit.

She fervently hoped that it hadn't been a premonition. If the chauffeur was here, who was to say that the Fantasy Travel representative hadn't come too.

Laura put her arms around the husky. He licked her cheek and buried his face in the crook of her arm. He wasn't a fan of air travel at all.

As the pilot tilted away from the volcano, the sun glinted off the white outline of a building. It was in the far north of the island, constructed partly on the cliffs and partly on a marina. The architect had designed it in such a way that the roof of the clifftop building was in the shape of the letter 'M', and the marina section spelled 'C'. Marine Concern, Laura guessed.

It was a baking hot afternoon but goosebumps rose on her arms. Was her uncle a prisoner in that sterile white building? Was he terrified? Hungry? In pain? Was he beside himself with worry, not knowing what had become of his niece and the boy with whose care he'd been entrusted? She and Tariq were going on nothing but guesswork. If they were wrong and her uncle was still in Antigua, precious time would be lost – time that could get him killed.

She nudged Tariq and pointed. There was a microphone attached to the bulky headphones that shielded their eardrums from the helicopter's machinegun roar, but she didn't want the pilot to hear her. Tariq gave her the thumbs up. He pressed his face against the glass door, straining to see something that might hint at what went on behind the walls. The sleek modern buildings and manicured lawns gave nothing away.

128

The pilot said into his mouthpiece: 'If you're wondering which company is brave enough, or idiotic enough, to erect their headquarters beside a volcano, it's a scientific research company called Marine Concern. They're on a mission to save rare sea life. There are a lot of rumours about them. The locals don't like it that they seldom offer islanders jobs, but if they're doing good work for endangered ocean species, I say we should leave them in peace.'

He steered the helicopter away from the volcano's menacing shadow. In no time at all they were landing at Montserrat's tiny airport. The pilot led them out of range of the spinning blades and escorted them into the terminal. The last flight of the day had just arrived. The low, cool building was buzzing with families and disoriented tourists trying to get their bearings. An aroma of coffee and conch burgers hung in the air, but the cafe had closed. A lone woman with a vacuum cleaner circled the tables like a bee collecting honey.

It was only now that Laura realised what an immense gamble they'd taken by leaving the relative sanctuary of the Blue Haven resort, where there was safety in numbers and they'd had free food and shelter. There was enough of Celia's money to pay for a couple of nights in a bed and breakfast on Montserrat, but none for a return ticket to Antigua. The free helicopter ticket had been for a volcano tour only. They'd had to do a lot of fast-talking to convince the pilot to drop them off in Montserrat. What they were going to do if they didn't find Calvin Redfern, she couldn't imagine. They hadn't thought further than getting to the island.

'You said you were doing the volcano tour for research purposes. What kind of research would that be?' the pilot was asking.

'It's top secret,' Laura told him, forcing a smile. 'It's to do with the case my uncle is working on. We could tell you but we'd have to kill you afterwards.'

He laughed. 'Where is your detective uncle? He's meeting you here, right? I'm curious to meet such a famous policeman. It'll be like encountering James Bond. Life and death, right?'

'That's right,' agreed Laura. 'Only thing is, he might be very late. My uncle, I mean. If he's held up with work, we could be here for hours and hours. We don't mind because we're used to it, but he certainly wouldn't expect you to do the same. Don't you have to get back to Antigua before nightfall?'

'It's highly likely that he'll be very, very late,' Tariq added, 'and he might also be in disguise. Especially if he's working undercover.'

It belatedly dawned on the pilot that there was something peculiar about two children and a husky travelling alone to Montserrat. 'Is that so? Well, I don't care if he's disguised as Donald Duck, I'm not leaving until he comes. There's no way I'm going to abandon a couple of kids on an island with an active volcano.'

'We'll definitely be okay,' Tariq insisted. 'You should get going. Thanks for all your help. We have money and we'll get a taxi if necessary.'

The pilot folded his arms across his chest. 'Okay, spit it out. You're in some kind of trouble, aren't you? There is no uncle, is there? I should have figured that out back in Antigua. That's it, I'm calling the police.'

He started towards a security guard, a sinewy Caribbean who was laughing into his mobile phone near the terminal exit.

'Wait!' cried Laura, but the pilot only turned to say: 'Don't move or you'll be in big trouble.'

'Laura, look,' Tariq said under his breath.

Laura followed his gaze to the double doors that separated the terminal from the runway. They opened briefly to admit a couple of smartly dressed aircrew. Behind them, heading across the tarmac, were the LeFevers' bodyguards.

Laura's heart began to pound. 'Tariq, I think we're in one of those devil and the deep blue sea situations again.'

At the terminal exit, the security guard had put away his phone and was frowning as he listened to the pilot's story. He took out his radio and spoke rapidly into it.

'We could make a run for it, but we wouldn't get very far,' Tariq said. 'On the other hand, if we wait here, we'll either be deported or end up as shark food, and who knows what'll happen to your uncle then. What do you reckon Matt Walker would do?'

The security guard was putting away his radio and fingering the handcuffs on his belt. Little and Large were having a heated debate and hadn't seen them yet, but that could change in a heartbeat. Laura pulled Skye and Tariq behind a potted tree. 'Matt Walker would create a diversion. Trouble is, someone's already doing that.'

Opposite them, a goateed, bespectacled young man in

a navy blue polo shirt and an orange firefighter jumpsuit, rolled down to the waist, was engaged in a heated discussion with the woman behind the counter of the Post Express – 'We Deliver'– booth.

'But you told me that if I made it here by five-thirty, it would be in Antigua by morning,' he cried passionately, brandishing a small box. 'You promised. And now you tell me you're closed.'

'I say five-turty and I mean five-turty,' the woman in the booth said placidly. 'Now it's five-turty-tree and we done shut up shop for da day.'

'But don't you understand, you're putting people's lives at stake. All for the sake of three lousy minutes. Are you happy to have that on your conscience? Do you have any idea what it's like to be swallowed by a pyroclastic flow? That's a flow of rock and gas travelling at 700kmph at 1,000 degrees Celsius, in case you're not familiar with the term. That's what could happen if this package doesn't get to Antigua on time.'

The bodyguards passed the potted tree, still arguing furiously. Laura caught the words, '. . . find those brats or we might as well throw ourselves . . .' She had not the slightest doubt that they were referring to her and Tariq.

'Here goes,' Tariq said, as the security guard and pilot strode purposefully towards them.

'I don't know about any pyromaniac whatsit,' Mrs Postal Express's voice boomed out across the terminal. 'Arl I know is dat you, Rupert, would be late ta yo own funeral. Every week we has dis same prublem. And every week you tell me, "Clara, for tree lousy minutes, or ten lousy minutes or twelve, why you making such a fuss? My samples need to get to Antigua yesterday or the volcano will go up in smoke and I won't be able to warn nobody." Nunsense. Now if you don't get yo hide outta my sight and back ta da Volcano Observatory, da only volcano on dis island is gonna be me.'

And with that, she wrenched down the steel shutter of her booth with a clatter and vanished from view.

'What's going on here?' demanded the security guard, advancing on the children aggressively. 'You kids ain't in any trouble with the law, are you? Mr Lynch here says der is nobody here to greet you, and dat ya gave him some cockeyed story about a detective uncle and a missing person. Dis sounds like a po-lees matter – '

But Laura wasn't listening. She was processing the conversation she'd just heard. Something clicked in her head.

'Rupert!' she cried, evading the security guard's hand and rushing over to the owl-like young man in the orange jumpsuit. 'We thought you'd forgotten us. I'm Laura and that's my husky, Skye and my best friend, Tariq, over by the tree. We're friends of Joshua. He did tell you we were coming, didn't he? He told us you'd help us.'

Rupert stared at her in bewilderment. 'What? Joshua? I haven't spoken to him in months. I guess he forgot to mention it.'

'But you will?' Laura said imploringly. 'Help us, I mean? You see, we're getting a hard time from those men over there. They don't believe that we're being met by an adult, and are threatening to turn us over to the police.'

Rupert scratched his head. 'How did you say you know Joshua?'

Laura was a nervous wreck, especially since Large had returned to the terminal. By the looks of things, he was demanding food from the cleaner in the cafe.

She shifted so her body was screened by Rupert's. 'We met Joshua in Antigua. He's the kindest man on earth. And he spoke very highly of you. He said you were a brilliant volcanologist.'

A broad smile brightened Rupert's open, boyish face. 'Did he really? He is the best man I know. And his wife could outcook any fancy chef.' He came to a decision. 'If Joshua sent you, of course I'll help. What do you need me to do?'

Large was on his way out of the terminal with two takeaway containers in his hand, a smug expression on his brutish face.

Laura led Rupert over to the group behind the palm. She gave Tariq a wink and murmured to the pilot: 'We did explain that my uncle might be in disguise. Sometimes even we struggle to recognise him.'

The pilot stared at Rupert as if he were James Bond come to life. The security guard looked crushed. If the children were being met by a responsible adult, there would be no arrest. His moment of importance had passed.

'Good evening, gentlemen,' said Rupert. 'What seems to be the problem here? Apologies if there's been any confusion. I was a bit tied up with a postal problem and didn't realise that Laura and Tariq had arrived.I'm going to be taking care of them while their detective uncle is busy solving a case here on the island. If you have any questions, please feel free to email me. Here is my card.'

~ 19 ~

'**HADN'T YOU BETTER** tell me what's going on?' said Rupert, in a soft Canadian accent, as they drove out of town in his battered truck.

Laura took a big breath of the air rushing by the window. The golden light of evening lent a rainbow glow to the gaily-painted houses slipping past. A boy playing with a puppy looked up and waved. Laura put her arms around Skye and waited for her heartbeat to slow. There'd been another near miss at the airport before they left. She and Tariq had managed to get into Rupert's Land Rover without been spotted by the bodyguards, but the husky had leapt out of the vehicle before they could shut the door, unable to resist chasing a cart loaded with goats and chickens.

Unfortunately Little and Large were still eating burgers in their black SUV at the time. Laura barely had a chance to say, 'If anybody asks, he's your dog,' to a startled Rupert, before bedlam erupted.

Crouching on the floor of the truck, she and Tariq heard Large demand: 'Where is the owner of this dog?'

Laura risked a peek over the dashboard. The volcanologist was not a small man, but the musclebound bodyguard dwarfed him.

Thankfully Rupert was not easily intimidated. 'He's my dog. Not that it's any of your business. Now if you'll excuse me . . .'

'Do I look like a moron?' Large boomed. 'Nobody in the Caribbean owns huskies, especially not three-legged ones. This husky belongs to Laura Marlin. She is a treacherous fugitive who is being hunted by the authorities. Anyone who aids her risks ending up in jail alongside her.'

On the Land Rover floor, Tariq put a protective arm around Laura, but they both knew that Rupert owed them nothing. Why should he risk jail or a beating for the sake of two children he'd known for all of twenty minutes?

Thankfully Rupert's loyalty to Joshua ran deep.

'In answer to your first question, all I'm going to say is: Have you looked in the mirror lately? Secondly, plenty of people own huskies in the Caribbean. There's a whole movie about a guy in Jamaica who races them. Thirdly, I've never heard of this Laura Marler woman. To be completely truthful, this dog was found abandoned and given to me by a friend of mine, but there's no way I'm parting with him until I have proof of previous ownership. Lastly, and this is very important. I've named my dog Vesuvius and if you don't wish to find out why, I'd advise you to step out of the way.'

Skye did his special, 'I-eat-polar-bears-for-breakfast' snarl. Within seconds Rupert was behind the wheel. The engine roared to life. Laura and Tariq climbed off the floor and did up their seatbelts, taking care to keep out of sight of passing traffic until they were well clear of the airport.

Rupert was the first to break the silence with his question.

When neither of them replied, he said: 'Okay, you have two minutes to tell me who you are and what exactly is going on, or I'm taking you back to the airport.'

Tariq said: 'I'll explain, sir.'

Rupert gave him an exasperated look. 'I'm not sir, I'm just plain Rupert. Go on then, spit it out.'

So Tariq told him everything. He explained about Calvin Redfern's fall and subsequent disappearance, about the Straight A gang, and about how he and Laura were brazenly kidnapped in full view of the *Ocean Empress* passengers, captain and security manager by Celia and Sebastian LeFever. The only thing he left out was their theory about Calvin Redfern being held captive by pirates connected to Marine Concern.

Rupert gave a low whistle. 'Well, either you're amazing liars and I'm about to get myself in hot water for harbouring two imposters, or you're two of the bravest kids I've ever met. I'm trusting my instincts that it's the latter. I'm not sure how I can help you though. The way I see it your uncle could be anywhere in the Caribbean, Laura. What makes you think he's on Montserrat? It would be a tough place to hide someone. The island community is very close-knit.'

'Just a hunch.'

'A hunch? You've flown all this way and almost got yourselves arrested for a hunch? You're not brave, you're crazy.'

'It was a bit more than a hunch,' Tariq admitted. 'One of the pirates dropped something on the *Ocean Empress* that we later found out was from Montserrat.'

'Look, you've no idea how grateful we are for what you're doing for us,' Laura said. 'I promise you can trust us. We did escape from the LeFevers and I'm not a "treacherous fugitive".'

Rupert kept his eyes on the road, but he was amused. 'I'd figured as much, Laura Marlin. I rather suspect it's the other way round. That bodyguard had the look of a wanted criminal if ever there was one.' He glanced at the rucksack – their only luggage. 'Now am I correct in thinking you've nowhere to stay?'

'To be honest, we haven't done much planning,' Tariq admitted. 'We'd appreciate it if you could point us in the right direction.'

Rupert grinned. 'What if I pointed you in the direction of the volcano?'

They'd been travelling west towards the sea, but now the coastal road snaked south towards the distant dark shape of the Soufriere Hills. Cloud concealed the top of it. The sky behind it was burnt orange with the setting sun.

'Just kidding,' he said. 'Volcanoes are my passion and

I often make the mistake of thinking other people are fascinated by them too, but . . .'

'I'm fascinated by them,' said Tariq. 'If we had more time I'd love to see this volcano up close.'

Rupert's eyes shone. 'Oh, you'd love my camp. It's in the foothills of the volcano . . .' He stopped. 'No, no, no, I'm absolutely not taking you there. No, we're going to do the sensible thing and continue along this nice tarmac road to the Blessing Guest House, the best bed and breakfast I know. There you'll be comfortable and in safe hands. I can lend you a little money if you need it.'

Laura and Tariq looked at each other and then up at the volcano, a black silhouette against the sunset. A scene from Laura's nightmare flashed through her mind. 'It's now or never,' the Fantasy Holidays rep was saying. 'She knows too much. Get rid of her.'

'No!' cried Laura.

She blinked. Tariq and Rupert were staring at her in surprise.

'You don't want to go to the bed and breakfast?' Rupert asked. 'I suppose I could try the hotel, but it's a lot more expensive.'

Laura swallowed. 'What I mean is, I know it's a lot to ask, but is there any chance we could stay with you? At your camp?'

She didn't add that the reason she was so keen to stay with him was because if his home was near the volcano, it was also near the offices of Marine Concern. That would make keeping an eye on their target a whole lot easier. Plus it would be free.

But he shook his head. 'It's too risky.' He turned off the main road into a village. Banana palms waved in the dusk. The sky behind them was turning vermillion. The air was smoky with the smell of sizzling fish and roasting corn. Laura's stomach rumbled. It seemed a long time since lunch.

'The geoscientists at MVO – that's the Montserrat Volcano Observatory - monitor the volcano constantly,' Rupert was saying. 'It's been very quiet for over a year now – too quiet if you ask me, but in recent weeks there have been signs of activity. In my opinion, it could flare up at any time. My camp is in the Exclusion Zone. Apart from the fact that it's illegal for anyone to enter the Exclusion Zone without permission, I've parked my caravan about as close to the volcano as it's possible to get without being boiled alive. My colleagues think I'm a madman. So, no, you're not staying with me. You're going to the Blessing Guest House.'

A rooster burst from the shadows and tore across the road. Rupert braked so hard the tyres squealed. The children's seatbelts slammed into their chests as they were propelled forward. Rupert went to move off again but his hand went still on the gearstick.

'Do you see what I see?' he said. Parked outside the Blessing Guest House, a rose-covered blue bungalow made enchanting by an abundance of swinging paper lanterns holding flickering candles, was the black SUV.

'What now?' cried Laura. 'If the Straight A's get their hands on us we'll never save my uncle.'

'Or ourselves,' Tariq pointed out.

141

Rupert gave them a hard look. 'The two of you are in a lot of trouble, aren't you? This is real, isn't it? I mean, at the airport it all seemed a bit of a game. Even the bodyguards, Little and Large, well, they're like cartoon baddies. When the bodybuilder one confronted me about Skye, I wasn't scared. I wanted to start laughing. But there's something about seeing their vehicle there, parked outside Mrs Blessing's guesthouse, that makes it real. It's menacing somehow. Threatening.'

'Look, Rupert, we'll understand if you don't want any part of this,' Laura said. 'Obviously we'd appreciate it if you don't leave us here, but you could perhaps drop us off at the hotel or back at the airport. Calvin Redfern is my uncle and we're strangers to you. Why should you risk your life or health for people you don't know? Go back to your volcano and forget you ever met us.'

Rupert gave a wry smile. 'That's just it. I can't. Don't you see, I'm already involved. I lied to a security guard who was about to call the police and have you arrested or at least taken into care. Doubtless the best thing would have been for me to do exactly that, but I didn't. I rescued you for the same reason I live within smoking distance of the volcano.'

'What's that?' Tariq wanted to know.

He laughed. 'I have an appetite for adventure.'

Then he became serious. 'Your uncle. He's in deadly danger, isn't he? Why don't we call the police? If he's a detective, the police will be his friends. They'll be only too glad to help.'

Laura paled. 'No police.'

Rupert sighed. 'What have I got myself into?'

The door of the Blessing Guest House opened and out came Little. He had his back to them and was talking to someone inside.

'Whatever we do, we need to do it quickly,' said Laura.

'We're going to Plan B,' said Rupert, executing a U-turn so rapid he only narrowly missed the rooster as it strutted across the road again. 'Tariq, you've got your wish. You'll be getting up close and personal with the volcano after all. Let's hope you don't get more than you bargained for. Although ironically the Exclusion Zone might prove the safest place for you.'

He slammed his boot down on the accelerator. The old Land Rover shot forward with a growl. 'Volcano, here we come.'

✫ ✫ ✫ ✫ ✫ ✫ ✫ ✫ ✫

20

IT WAS DARK when they reached Rupert's home in the Soufriere foothills, having made a detour along the way to get a permit to enter the Exclusion Zone. The man at the permit office had asked a lot of questions, but Rupert had given them the story that Laura and Tariq were his godchildren, out for a rare visit from St Ives, Cornwall. He would, he promised, keep them from harm.

'I hope I'm not tempting fate by saying that,' Rupert murmured as they bumped up the rough track. The volcano loomed over them, a brooding black hill that reminded Laura of photos she'd seen of Mount Kilimanjaro in Africa. Before turning off the engine, Rupert backed the

Land Rover up to the caravan and connected the tow hitch. Moths swirled in the headlights' white glow.

'Volcano Safety Rule No.1: Be prepared for a quick getaway,' he said, switching on a torch to unlock the caravan door. 'Volcano Safety Rule No.2: Never take anything for granted.'

He winked when he said it, but it was obvious he was deadly serious. Butterflies fluttered in Laura's stomach. She and Tariq were gambling everything on a cheap tin badge, which might not even belong to one of the pirates. A picture of Jimmy's expression as she pressed it into his palm came into her mind. Something had flickered in his bright, enquiring eyes. She'd been sure that he understood that she wanted him to do some investigating. But almost immediately that expression had been replaced by confusion and disappointment. Now she suspected it had only been wishful thinking on her part.

Besides, he was a ten-year-old boy. Once he was having fun at some idyllic Caribbean resort, he'd forget all about them.

'Welcome to my humble abode.' Rupert threw open the door and flicked a switch. Warm lamplight revealed a compact but surprisingly homely space. There were CDs strewn messily on a table, postcards and family photos pinned on a board next to the fridge, and laundry piled on a chair. An old-fashioned poster of Mount Etna hung on the wall. The most striking thing in the caravan was a display of starfish of all different colours and sizes.

Rupert noticed Laura staring at them. 'Before you ask, I didn't buy those. I'm extremely opposed to the sale of endangered marine creatures. I found them on a deserted beach on the southern tip of the island. There is no way that so many unusual species of starfish could have washed up on the shore by chance, so they must have been dropped by a smuggler. I returned to the beach every day for the rest of the week, but saw nothing suspicious. The Marine Concern researchers I bumped into on one trip said they'd keep an eye out for any illegal activity.'

'Marine Concern?' Laura burst out before she could stop herself.

Rupert was surprised. 'Yes. Why, have you heard of them?'

'We talked to a waitress wearing a Marine Concern T-shirt when we were in Antigua,' Laura said. 'They save dolphins or something, don't they?'

'Not exactly. They research rare marine species and look into ways of saving them. Their offices and laboratories are at the foot of the cliffs a couple of kilometres away. The Montserrat Volcano Observatory staff tried to talk them out of building their offices in the path of the volcano, but they were adamant that that specific location was essential for their research. It has the safest harbour on the island or some such thing. I attempted to interest them in signing up to Project V, the eruption early warning system I'm developing, but they were hostile to say the least. They said they had their own state-of-the-art monitoring system in place.'

Laura said nothing. The more she heard about Marine Concern, the more she was convinced they had something to hide.

It turned out that the caravan slept four. Tariq and Laura

chose the foldout bunk beds in the living room area. Skye settled on the mat by the door. He'd been cooped up since mid-afternoon in a motorised bird and a ratty old Land Rover, and he was dying to go out exploring.

'After dinner,' Laura promised him in a whisper, hoping that there was food somewhere in the caravan.

Rupert flung open the fridge. 'Guava juice okay?' he said, pouring them two big glasses before they had time to answer. 'Hungry? Of course you are. You must be starving. Well, I can offer you fried Mountain Chicken, a local speciality, which is not chicken but frogs' legs, absolutely delicious. What, you don't fancy it? Or I have Goat Water – a Montserratian goat meat stew.'

Laura spluttered: 'Umm, thanks very much but I'm not hungry.'

'We just ate,' Tariq agreed.

'Just ate when?' Rupert said. 'Back in Antigua about eight hours ago?' He grinned. 'Oh, I get it. You're vegetarian but too polite to tell me. Don't worry, I'll rustle something up. You're going to need your strength if we're going to start going door to door in Montserrat hunting for your uncle.'

Laura, who really was starving, could have wept with relief, especially since Rupert prepared a pot of peas (black-eyed beans) and rice in no time at all on his little gas stove. He served it up with buttered spinach, hot sauce, and more guava juice.

When the meal was ready, the trio dined by candlelight beneath the dark mass of the volcano and a ceiling winking stars. Had her uncle not been missing, Laura would have found the experience nothing short of magical.

Silence enveloped them like a balm. The only sound was Skye licking his chops under the wooden table. He was decidedly not a vegetarian and had gobbled the Goat Water stew with relish.

'Have you always been interested in volcanoes?' Tariq asked Rupert.

The volcanologist laughed. 'Always. My mum claims that when I was a toddler she could keep me quiet for hours by showing me the volcano section in *Encyclopedia Britannica*. But I'm obsessed by this volcano in particular.'

Laura tipped more hot sauce onto her beans. 'Why?'

'Because it's unique. No other volcano has had such a devastating effect on the community around it. You see, before it erupted in July 1995 it had been dormant for 400 years. The Montserratians had come to love their volcano; had believed that it would always be this beautiful, but benign feature of their Emerald Isle. The first sign that they were very much mistaken was a phreatic explosion.'

'Free what?' asked Tariq between mouthfuls.

'Phrea-a-tic. It might be easier for you to remember it as free-a-tick. Most people think of volcanoes as spewing molten streams of lava. Some do, but others spit out terrifying streams of rocks and steam, which reach temperatures of over 1,000 degrees and barrel down the outer walls of the volcano like fiery express trains. You might have seen the consequences on your helicopter trip – Montserrat's capital city and its old airport buried under forty feet of mud.'

He paused to pour them each a cup of milky coffee from a flask. Laura took a sip. It had a smoky flavour.

'Go on,' encouraged Tariq.

'Next, a dome formed. That's when magma – molten rock – pushes upwards and causes the land to balloon with the pressure. You'd imagine that would cause an explosion, but it does the opposite. A couple of years later, the collapse of the dome triggered the first of many pyroclastic flows. Pyroclastic means "fire rock". An easy way to remember it is to think of it as a "glowing cloud". It's a lethal mix of lava, hot rocks and gas. It's impossible to outrun it, as those who'd stayed found to their cost.'

'Joshua told us about that,' Tariq said.

'Yes,' added Laura. 'He also mentioned something about dancing skeletons.'

Rupert's mouth twisted. 'I'm aware that Joshua's wife and several other people have seen what they thought were dancing skeletons on the slopes of the volcano, but my caravan has been parked in this spot for eighteen months now and I never have. I'm not saying they're making things up, but . . .'

'But what?' pressed Laura.

'Put it this way. I'm a scientist. I believe that everything – including ghostly apparitions – has a scientific explanation. As far as I'm concerned, there is no such thing as supernatural.'

He covered his mouth to hide a yawn. 'Now I don't know about you, but I'm tuckered out after all the excitement. How about we hit the hay?'

One legacy of his former existence as a quarry slave was that Tariq slept as lightly as a cat. At 1.16am Skye made a soft 'gruff' sound in his throat. The Bengali boy was on his feet and fully alert almost before the sound had faded.

He dressed silently, clipped on the husky's lead and slipped out into the night. He and Laura had planned to exercise Skye after dinner, but in the end had been too exhausted. They'd barely had the energy to fall into their bunk beds. Tariq felt guilty. The dog did so love to run.

For that reason, he had no objection as Skye pulled him along the hill path. The track was uneven and covered in loose shale, and several times Tariq nearly lost his footing as he hurried to keep up.

'Slow down, Skye,' he pleaded, but still the husky strained forward. His ears were pricked and he was focused and intent. Something was driving him on.

They rounded a bend and a powerful gust of wind nearly blew Tariq off balance. Only Skye's sudden stop anchored him. He looked down. Directly beneath him was the observation deck Rupert and the other scientists used to monitor the volcano. On the edge of the distant cliffs, lights spelled out the initials of Marine Concern. Beyond was the shifting dark sea, streaked metallic blue by the moonlight. Three fishing boats were moving in a line towards the horizon.

'Grrrr,' went Skye.

Tariq just about leapt out of his skin. On the rocky face of the volcano, barely fifty yards from him, six ghostly skeletons danced. Their bones gave off an unearthly white glow. As they bumped and jived to silent music, their skulls wobbled on their knobbly spines and they bared their teeth in grim grins.

Most children would have run screaming for home, but Tariq was no ordinary boy. In his eleven years on the planet, he'd seen and experienced things that would have reduced a grown man to tears, and he'd learned that courage, calmness and meditation could get him through most things. Unlike the volcanologist, Tariq did believe in a spirit world. Unlike Joshua's wife, he was not afraid of it.

Once he'd recovered from the initial shock, he stood with his hand on Skye's collar watching the skeletons' surreal dance. When their bony frames faded from view, he walked back to the caravan deep in thought. It was 2am when he finally crawled into his bunk. Not even ghosts could keep him from sleep.

'**A 3D HOLOGRAM?**' Laura said the next morning. They were sitting at the wooden table under an ominous grey sky, eating French toast dripping with maple syrup. 'You mean to say that there are no ghosts? That someone with a computer and a projector is beaming dancing skeletons onto the volcano for fun.'

'I'm willing to believe it,' Rupert said. 'I told you that the explanation would be a scientific one.'

Tariq stirred sugar into his coffee, wrapping his hands around his cup for extra warmth. 'Not for fun, for a reason. To frighten people away.'

Rupert laughed. 'Who would they be trying to frighten?

There are only 5,000 people left on Montserrat and 99 per cent of those live in the north of the island around Little Bay, many miles from here. The rest work at Marine Concern. Apart from myself, the occasional scientist and tour groups photographing the volcano – and they're only around during the day, there *is* nobody to frighten. Who would want to frighten people with skeletons anyway? That's silly.'

'Not if you want to distract them,' Laura pointed out, recalling a Matt Walker case where a murderous magician had used a projected image of a couple at an upstairs window to fool neighbours into thinking there were two people in an apartment at a time when one was already dead. 'Not if there's something you want to hide.'

'That's what I think,' Tariq said. 'At the exact time that the skeletons started dancing, I saw three fishing boats leaving the harbour at Marine Concern.'

Rupert ran his hand over the blond stubble on his jaw. Laura could see that he wanted to believe them, but didn't. 'Marine Concern? What do they have to do with anything? And the bay is full of fishing boats – hundreds of them.' He pushed his plate away. 'Hold on – you know something, don't you? You were asking questions about Marine Concern last night. Is this about your missing uncle? What's going on?'

They were forced to tell him then. Forced to admit that they'd come to Montserrat on a wing and a prayer, on the off chance that Calvin Redfern was being held captive at Marine Concern.

Rupert was incredulous. 'That's the wildest thing I've

ever heard. Why would an institute devoted to saving rare sea life kidnap your uncle?'

'Maybe they're not as devoted as they make out,' Tariq said. 'Maybe saving sea life is a front for something else.'

'It still doesn't explain why they'd be projecting ghostly skeletons onto the mountain when there's no one around to see them,' Rupert responded. 'Guys, I think you're making a big mistake. And, as you rightly point out, every minute lost is a minute cost in terms of searching for Mr Redfern. I don't know what you've got against the police.'

'The police bungle everything,' Laura said, using a phrase she'd borrowed from Matt Walker. 'Not all detectives are as dedicated as my uncle. Besides, we don't have time for that. This is an emergency situation. We have to find a way to at least check out Marine Concern.'

'Good luck with that. That place has more guards than a maximum security prison. They have an area for the general public, which you can visit with no problem, but you have absolutely no chance of seeing behind the scenes. I know because I went there to try to talk to them about my Volcano Early Warning System. They treated me like an escaped lunatic.'

He hesitated. 'There is another way . . .'

Tariq learned forward eagerly. 'What other way?'

'An old lava tunnel that runs under their offices. There might be a way to at least spy on things from there. No, scratch that. Bad idea. Don't look at me like that. I'm not aiding and abetting you in any criminal activities and you can forget about talking me into it.' He stopped. 'Is that an engine I hear?'

A postal van came bumping up the rough track. The driver handed Rupert a package postmarked Antigua. 'Hey mate. Dis da information you be waiting for?'

Rupert tore the envelope in his eagerness to open it. 'I'll tell you in a minute.' But when he'd read the contents he went still and said nothing.

'What is it?' asked Laura. 'Is something wrong?'

But Rupert was miles away. She had to repeat the question twice before he said distractedly: 'What? Oh, umm, I don't know, to be honest. I need to go to the observation platform to take a few readings. The keys to the caravan are in the door. Make yourselves at home. I'll see you shortly. Promise me you won't go anywhere without me.'

'Promise,' Laura said, but she was talking to thin air. Rupert was already running up the path that led to the volcano. He paused briefly to yell: 'Thanks, Jack,' before disappearing from view.

The postman shrugged. 'Dese volcano scientists, day arl got one or two screws loose if you know what I mean.' He was gone in a plume of dust.

'What was that all about?' Laura asked as they gathered up the breakfast things. At the caravan's tiny sink, Tariq washed as she dried. Skye was dozing on the mat. Rupert had taken him on his early morning run and for once the husky was worn out.

'I'm not sure, but it seemed serious,' Tariq said. 'He was telling me about his Early Warning system. He and a couple of earth scientists in Antigua have been working on a project to detect minute changes in soil chemistry that can predict an eruption up to five hours before even the most advanced computer monitoring system. With volcanoes, every minute counts, so that could save a lot of lives. If the delivery is from Antigua, it might mean the volcano is about to blow.'

'Great,' said Laura. 'That's all we need on top of everything else. As soon as Rupert returns, we need to persuade him to tell us where this lava tunnel begins and ends. Since we can't exactly visit the public area of Marine Concern, we need to find another way in.'

She wiped her hands on the tea towel. 'Do you think Rupert is right about the skeletons? Why would anyone project skeleton holograms onto a mountain when there's hardly anyone around to see them? Rupert has been here eighteen months and he hasn't seen them once.'

'But I saw them,' Tariq said. 'So did Joshua's wife. What if they're not directed at anyone in particular? What if they only appear if there's something secret going on at Marine Concern – a mission involving the fishing boats, for instance? Maybe the skeletons are projected at the volcano as a precaution just in case someone happens to be around.'

Adrenalin surged into Laura's veins. 'And who's more likely to do something like that than the Straight A's. Tariq, we're on to something big, I know we are. Maybe my uncle's been kidnapped because he stumbled on to a major plot.'

There was a noise outside. She dried her hands and looked out of the window. In the short space of time they'd been inside, the weather had turned ugly. It seemed to her that the volcano was smoking, but cloud veiled the top of the hills and it was hard to tell. The caravan rocked in the wind. The door slammed shut.

Skye leapt to his feet, barking. Laura hushed him. She went to open the door and was surprised to find it wouldn't budge. Tariq threw his weight against it, but it was stuck.

Laura returned to the window. She suddenly became aware of an odd, medicinal smell in the caravan and she wanted to air it out. She tried to undo the latch, but it needed a key. All of a sudden she was too exhausted to hunt for one. She was about to ask Tariq to help when she spotted the corner of a van. 'Hey, we're in luck. The postman is back again. If we yell, he'll let us out.'

But Tariq was incapable of yelling for anyone. He was climbing into his bunk as feebly as an old man. 'I'm so sorry, Laura,' he said groggily. 'I can't keep my eyes open.' To Laura's astonishment, his head slumped on the pillow and he began to snore.

Skye was lying on his side near the door, eyes shut, dead to the world.

Laura's knees threatened to give way beneath her. She fell into a chair. She registered that something was very wrong, but her brain had turned to cotton wool and she was incapable of doing anything about it. Her vision blurred. A black snake, or perhaps it was a tube, was dangling from an air vent. 'Gas,' she thought weakly. Her eyelids drooped.

The door opened and the bodyguards burst in. The thin, ghoulish face of Little peered down at her, like the

Grim Reaper. 'You and your associates have caused a lot of trouble to a lot of people, Miss Marlin,' he said. 'But your days of making mischief are over. Say goodbye to the good life.'

21

'**HOW WOULD YOU** like to win a Caribbean cruise to an island with sand so white it sparkles – an island with three hundred and sixty-five beaches, one for every day of the year. Picture yourself in paradise. Imagine lying in a hammock sipping coconut milk while dolphins . . .'

Laura willed her eyes to open. Her eyelids were so heavy it was as if they'd been stitched together, yet even in the depths of the fog clouding her brain she knew that her survival depended on her being alert. She was in a bare room containing nothing but two mattresses, two plastic beakers of water and a chair, now occupied by the Fantasy Holidays travel representative.

Tariq was sitting cross-legged on the second mattress, watching the woman. His expression said: 'My hands might be bound and you might be twice my size and hold all the power, but it would be unwise of you to underestimate me.'

There was no sign of Skye.

'You lied to me,' Laura said.

The woman tossed her head like a horse and laughed. She had close-cropped blonde hair and a lean, muscular frame. Olive green cargo trousers, combat boots and a black T-shirt had replaced her Fantasy Holidays uniform.

'You're a liar,' Laura said again.

'Not at all. Every word was true. You did, as promised, win a luxury cruise to the Caribbean. You did go to a paradise island with three hundred and sixty-five beaches and turquoise waters. According to the hotel records, you ordered coconut milk to drink. It's your own fault if you chose not to lie in a hammock. As for the dolphins, we have a couple here. I'm sure we could arrange a quick swim for you before . . . well, let's say, before our plans for you unfold . . .

'The only teensy weensy white lie I told was the bit about the Siberian husky. I never did like dogs. Worked a treat, though. I do believe that that was the part that convinced you to buy a ticket. We left the husky behind, by the way. He woke up unexpectedly and turned ugly. I believe one of our men was considering eliminating him when he ran away.'

She stretched like a cat. 'I should introduce myself. I'm Janet Rain. Not my real name, naturally, but it'll do.'

Laura wriggled upright. She flexed her numb hands in a bid to loosen the tape around her wrists. Pins and needles prickled in them. 'You know perfectly well that, thanks to you and the rest of the Straight A gang, we've had the holiday from hell. What I want to know is why? Why did you go to so much trouble when you could have just kidnapped us in St Ives? And what have you done with my uncle? I want to see him. If you've hurt him, I'm going to devote the rest of my life to tracking you all down and sending you one by one to the worst prisons on earth.'

Janet Rain laughed delightedly. 'You're quite a little character – you and your silent friend here. It's almost a shame to get rid of you. You're a regular Matt Walker.'

'You haven't answered Laura's question,' said Tariq, speaking for the first time. 'Why did you do it? Why go to the effort of luring us to the Caribbean when you could have snatched us in Cornwall?'

Her gaze fixed on him. 'For the game, of course. That's half the fun. You see, the Straight A's believe the punishment should fit the crime. Ex-Chief Inspector Redfern has committed two grave sins—'

'What sins?' cried Laura. 'You're the criminal, not him.'

'That's a matter of perspective, my dear. Quite apart from the fact that Calvin Redfern – with the aid of you and your boyfriend here – has sent several of our most talented operatives to jail, he was in the process of disrupting our Atlantic Bluefin Tuna operation, potentially costing us tens of millions of dollars. We couldn't allow that.'

Laura was stunned. 'That's what all of this is about – tuna fish?'

Janet waved a brown hand. 'Among other things. Bluefin tuna are on the road to extinction. Yet people still love to eat them. Think about it – when did you last go into a café that didn't sell tuna fish sandwiches? And it's a sushi bar staple. That's good for us because it drives up the prices.'

'Fewer fish mean more money,' Tariq said.

Janet looked at him. 'Smart boy. One good tuna can earn us $185,000. The black market is worth $7 billion annually. You can imagine how upset we were when Chief Inspector Redfern started meddling. Although, ironically, that made it easier to get you all here. When he didn't call right away to confirm your travel arrangements, we realised that he might be suspicious that a free holiday was a con. So we sent one of our best men to see him in the dead of night, claiming to have information on marine smuggling on a massive scale in Montserrat. Your uncle took the bait, hook, line and sinker.'

Laura said: 'That's because it was true, wasn't it? That's what you do here. You trade in rare marine species while pretending to be a conservation organization trying to save them. That's sick.'

Janet bounced to her feet with a grin. 'No, that's business genius. There are billions to be made out of endangered marine species. People focus on the cute and cuddly things – snow leopards, pandas, gorillas. They forget about the sea creatures. Nobody ever fell in love with a starfish or a tuna. If there was one less shark in the sea, who'd care?'

There was a long silence. Laura thought of her classmates back in St Ives. Most of them thought of sharks as marauding man-eaters that should be killed before they ripped you to pieces. And Janet was right about nobody loving starfish or tuna. Until her uncle had told her that tuna fish were on the verge of extinction, Laura had eaten dozens of tuna sandwiches without a qualm.

'You still haven't told us why you've brought us to the Caribbean,' Tariq said. 'What did you mean when you said the punishment should fit the crime?'

Janet rang a bell and the bodyguards appeared. 'I think,' she said, 'it's time for a tour.'

The C-shaped marina was a floating aquarium concealed by a white roof. The sound and smell of the sea was everywhere, pouring in through open vents. Escorted by Little and Large, the children were forced to follow Janet Rain as she walked the length of it, explaining the fate of each creature as they walked.

In the furthest tank were seahorses. They were the most angelic, pretty things Laura had ever seen. They bobbed sweetly in the water, oblivious to the terrible end in store for them.

'By this time tomorrow they'll be freeze-dried, packaged and on their way to Beijing,' Janet said. 'With over twenty-five million of them traded a year, they're real money-spinners. No trouble either.'

Laura and Tariq looked at each other. Neither of them spoke.

Next came several tanks of turtles, their shells like works

of art, followed by banks of pulsing coral and coloured ribbons in the shape of mythical animals. It was only when she saw them moving in slow duets, like dancers, that Laura realised they were alive.

'Weedy and leafy seadragons from Australia,' Janet informed them. 'Seahorse family. Nature's miracle. Much prized by collectors.'

They'd reached the end of the first section. Little spoke into a radio and a steel gate opened. Janet gave them a malevolent grin. 'And now for the monsters.'

'I thought they were already here,' Laura said, but her words bounced off Janet Rain like rubber bullets off a steel tank.

They passed through a door and Laura bit back a gasp. They were on a narrow walkway. On either side of them a row of giant tanks, each as big as an Olympic swimming pool, held dozens of sharks of different species. A Great White poked its head out of the water and sniffed the air.

'Watch your step,' warned Large. 'You might fall in and then it would be dinner time.' He made a ghastly crunching sound and licked his lips.

Janet Rain giggled. 'You are a tease, Mr Pike.'

She turned to Laura and Tariq. 'All those summer movies about tourists being gobbled by Great Whites with jaws as big as caves are fabulous publicity for the Straight A's business. Guess how many people are killed by sharks each year? Around four. You have more chance of being struck dead by a falling coconut. Sharks don't like eating humans. However, humans love eating sharks. Nearly a hundred million are killed every year, mainly for shark fin soup, a Chinese delicacy. Some are sold as "rock salmon" in British fish and chip shops. 'Course, the sharks we have here are mainly rare species like spiny dogfish and oceanic whitetip, and therefore much more valuable.'

She paused. 'Naturally, these large fish are demonstration models only. Customers view them, place their orders and then our boats go out to hunt them. We believe we have the most sophisticated fish tracking sonar in the world. If you know what to look for, sea creatures are basically swimming money. Take those dolphins over there. People will pay anything to swim with dolphins. We capture them, train them and pack them off to theme parks.'

A blue pool with a variety of toys beside it held two listless dolphins. A trainer was trying to interest them in a bucket of dead fish.

'Damian, make them do a trick,' yelled Janet.

The trainer straightened. Laura recognised him immediately as the tall pirate from the ship, the one who had tried to coax her into the laundry hamper. He was no longer wearing his pirate regalia, but his sneer was unmistakable. He blew a whistle and one of the dolphins obediently turned a triple somersault. A strong stench of chlorine rose from the pool.

Laura fought back tears. 'You're inhuman,' she screamed at Janet. 'You and everyone else in the Straight A gang. You're barbarians.'

Tariq put his arm around her, causing Little to give him a shove. 'Don't let them get to you. We'll get out of here and we'll get justice.'

'You will get justice,' said Janet Rain, overhearing him.

'Indeed you will. That's why we've brought you all the way to the Caribbean. We've brought you here to teach you a lesson you'll never forget, Laura Marlin. We've brought you here to watch Calvin Redfern die.'

23

'**WHAT I DON'T** understand is why this sudden obsession with fish,' Rita Gannet said as Jimmy returned to the short video on octopi and their young for the third time. 'You've never shown the slightest interest in any sea creature in your life. Now they're so important to you that we've had to leave our fabulous Antiguan resort, a place with every conceivable form of entertainment, to come to Montserrat. If it were the volcano you wanted to see, that would be one thing. But no, you had to come to this fish research place. What is it called again?'

'Marine Concern. Mum, look at how incredible she is. I thought octopi were like blobs of jelly, but this octopus mum is the most loving mother in the sea.'

'When do we see the man-eating sharks, that's what I want to know,' Bob roared. 'What time's this tour thing? Ten a.m.?'

The visitors' museum attendant, a pale woman with glasses and hair tightly bound in a bun, regarded him with thinly veiled dislike. 'I'm sorry to disappoint you, sir, but I'm afraid all aquarium tours have been cancelled for the day.'

Bob advanced on her. 'You cannot be serious. Have you any idea how much it has cost us to fly to Montserrat? A king's ransom, that's how much. The flight was so bumpy I almost lost my breakfast, and let's not get started on the taxi from the airport. Fleeced we were, absolutely fleeced. I'm surprised he didn't ask for my watch. And after all that you want to break the heart of my boy, Jimmy.'

The attendant was impassive. 'I apologise for the inconvenience, sir, but it's out of my hands.'

'This is an outrage,' Bob said. 'Why weren't we told? I want my money back. Rita, are you hearing this?'

'What, dear?' Rita mumbled from the depths of a sensory experience booth. She had pressed the button marked Hunting Turtle. 'Ooooh weeeh, Bob, you need to feel this to believe it.'

Jimmy held tightly to the badge in his pocket. His mind was racing. It had taken considerable effort to convince his parents to leave their magnificent resort and take a day trip to Montserrat, all so he could visit a sea life research facility, something that at first they'd refused point blank to consider.

He'd spent an equal number of hours scheming how to free Laura and Tariq if they had, as he suspected, been kidnapped. The aquarium tour had been key to that. And all the time, he was haunted by the thought that they might have spun him a pack of tall tales. That Laura's detective uncle might be a complete fiction and that the badge might mean nothing at all. It might have been Laura's feeble way of saying sorry for letting him down.

But the thing he returned to time and time again was how they'd saved his life – or at the very least saved him a trip to the hospital, at the adventure centre. They'd also kept their word about keeping him company on the ship, and had gone out of their way to include him, even when he sensed they'd rather have been alone. That's why he'd been so determined to be the detective he'd boasted he could become and do his best to help them. He'd spent ages on the internet at the resort figuring out where Marine Concern were located and how on earth to persuade his parents to take him there.

And after all that, here was this museum attendant, a woman with a face like a prison guard, telling them the aquarium tour was cancelled. She didn't look in the least bit sorry. He had the feeling that she enjoyed ruining their day.

It wasn't hard to make himself cry. All he had to do was imagine what would become of Laura and Tariq if he couldn't help them.

'I want to see the sharks,' he sobbed. 'Miss, I want to see the sharks. Please, miss, let me see the sharks.'

'Sorry, kid, the sharks are out of bounds today,' said the attendant, trying unsuccessfully to hide a scowl. She didn't like children at the best of times and this boy with the wild hair and T-shirt so vividly stained it was practically an artwork was no exception. 'Try the volcano. It's much more exciting.'

Jimmy stopped blubbing. He sniffed and said: 'Either you let me do the aquarium tour or I'll tell people that Marine Concern is a front for some shady operation and that you kidnap small children.'

Her face went the colour of marble and her mouth dropped open. 'I don't know what you . . . Who's been saying . . . ? What are you talking about? That's rubbish. Do you hear me? It's garbage.'

'Keep your wig on,' said Jimmy. 'I was only joking.'

'What's going on here?' demanded Bob, marching up. 'Have you made my boy cry? Jimmy, son, did this nasty person make you cry?'

With immense effort, the attendant summoned a smile. 'I was just explaining to your son that the aquarium tour is cancelled indefinitely for health and safety reasons. I appreciate that he is bitterly disappointed, so I'd like to make it up to him by giving him a gift.'

She took a cellophane wrapped package from a drawer and made a great fuss of presenting it to him. 'On behalf of Marine Concern, I'd like to apologise for inconveniencing you and present you with this as a token of our goodwill. Hopefully we'll be able to host you on an aquarium tour on another occasion.' Under her breath she said: 'Here, have a clean T-shirt, kid. You look as if you need one.'

Jimmy grinned. 'Cool, thanks. You're a nice lady. Well, maybe not nice exactly but . . . smart. Don't worry, I won't say anything about Marine Concern being a shady operation and . . .'

The attendant hissed like a snake. 'Shhh.'

Rita came rushing over, face aglow with the turtle experience. 'That was awesome. You should try it, Bob.'

'Not on your life. Come on, doll, let's get out of here. Jimmy, where are you going to now?'

'To the bathroom. I want to try on my new T-shirt.'

'Quick as you can. We're leaving shortly.'

Jimmy did indeed go to the bathroom, a door at the end of a long corridor marked by a shark wearing a tuxedo. But on his return he paused at an unmarked door. It was locked. Jimmy took out his mum's supermarket points card, which he'd taken the liberty of removing from her bag earlier, and inserted it into the space between the lock and the door. He'd studied the exact method on the Internet at the resort. Unfortunately, it didn't work quite as it had in the demonstration, or as it so easily worked in the movies. In actuality it didn't work at all.

Down the passage, his mum and dad were arguing with the attendant over the cancelled tour. Jimmy felt a failure as a detective. He'd been so sure that the card would work and he'd be able to burst in and heroically save his friends if, of course, they were there. But once again he was just bumbling, scruffy, hopeless Jimmy Gannet. That's how the kids thought of him at school. Oh, sure he was good at maths, science and pretty much every other subject. But in the playground and on the sports field, his classmates avoided him as if he was toxic waste. Unless they were bullying him.

In his head he was a lion, but in his heart he was . . . well, a mouse.

His heart pounded. What would Laura do?

Into his head came the advice she'd given him, about how Matt Walker said that a common weakness of criminals was being too clever for their own good. They were so obsessed with detail that they overlooked the ordinary things.

There was a squeak of wheels and a man came round the corner with a trolley heaped with towels and uniforms. Jimmy squatted down and pretended he was trying to get a stone out of his shoe.

The man nodded at him. ''Scuse us, 'scuse us.' Seizing a handle set into the wall, he dumped the laundry down a chute. The trolley squeaked away.

'Jimmy, what's taking you so long?' called his father.

Jimmy looked at the chute. He hadn't a clue where it ended, but he was hopeful that the laundry would provide a soft landing.

'JIMMY!'

Jimmy glanced quickly over both shoulders and opened the chute. It was difficult to clamber into and painful, since it had a sharp metal edge. While he was struggling to find something to hold onto, he lost his balance and fell headfirst. He had to grit his teeth to stop himself screaming all the way down.

24

MR PIKE GAVE Laura a shove that almost sent her flying. Tariq steadied her and gave the big bodyguard a warning glare.

'Ooh, I'm scared,' teased Large. 'I'm quaking in my boots.'

They were in a large white room at the halfway point of the aquarium, one whole side of which was a full-length window showing a cinematic stretch of grey-green sea. Storm clouds hung low over the churning waves. Pelicans dive-bombed leaping fish. Laura envied them their freedom.

'They've no idea we're prisoners,' she thought. 'No idea that the humans in this place are plotting to destroy the sea creatures they live on. And us.'

Janet flicked a switch and the storm-darkened room was illuminated. There were two swimming pools in it, a large one which, judging by the coloured balls and hoops, had been used as a dolphin training or display area. The other pool was close to the window. It was the size of a large Jacuzzi, but it wasn't bubbling. Instead, a red chair was suspended above it. Tied to the chair and looking very much paler and thinner than when they last saw him was Calvin Redfern.

Laura's mouth opened but no sound came out. She tried to rush forward, but the bodyguards held her in an iron grip. 'Uncle Calvin!'

Calvin Redfern's head snapped up. Relief, joy, panic and terror flitted across his face. 'Laura! Tariq! What are you doing here? No, don't answer that.'

He turned on Janet. 'Have you gone stark staring mad, Rain? They're *children*. Take your revenge on me. Do your worst and see if I care. But hurt my niece and Tariq at your peril. They've done nothing. They're innocent victims in your grudge match, your *war*, against me.'

'Innocent?' scoffed Sebastian LeFever. The man in white was crossing the grey tiles towards them, followed by his wife. 'After the dance they've led us across Antigua and Montserrat. After their dog bit my chauffeur and caused the wreck of my limousine, the ruination of my wife's dress, and a visit to A&E for us all. Please, spare me the "all children are angels" speech. In the three days since we met Laura Marlin and her friend, my wife and I have aged ten years.'

Laura stole a glance at Celia LeFever. She didn't look as

174

if she'd aged ten minutes. She could have stepped from the pages of a celebrity magazine. Calvin Redfern, on the other hand, was haggard and tense. She doubted he'd slept in days.

'Now that we're all here, let's get on with the game,' Janet said with relish. 'It's been fun so far – what with the tripwire, the pirates and the climbing wall prank, but the best is yet to come. She pressed a button and Calvin Redfern's chair whirred downwards until his bare feet were touching the water.

It was only then that Laura noticed a spiny, balloon-shaped fish, a blue-spotted octopus the size of a golf ball, an ugly grey creature that resembled a dirty rock, and a collection of snails dotted around the pool.

'Rutger, would you step forward and explain why you've chosen these particular species for our "fun-in-the-pool" session,' Janet ordered.

A swarthy man in oilskin trousers and a black fisherman's jumper stepped forward. He would have been handsome if his face hadn't been so cruel. He nodded at Calvin Redfern as casually as if he'd been passing him on the street.

'For a famous ex-detective, you were pretty easy to fool,' he remarked. 'You swallowed that tuna information like a pelican gulping down a fish. I almost felt sorry for you.'

'I'd enjoy a good laugh at my expense while you can,' Calvin Redfern said. 'When the tables turn, which they will, I'll be doing the same, only for a lot longer. How much do you think you'll get for kidnapping two children and a former policeman, Rutger? Ten years? Twenty? Life?'

Rutger grinned. 'I'll say this for you, ex-Chief Inspector. You're an optimist.' He picked up a steel rod and prodded each creature in turn.

'Right, here we have the pufferfish, one of the most poisonous creatures on earth. If all else fails, we're going to feed it to you at a banquet this evening.' He gave the spiky ball a prod. The frightened fish immediately ballooned to almost three feet in diameter. Laura was sure it was going to pop.

'After poisoning, victims experience a deadening of the tongue and lips, dizziness, rapid heart rate and finally muscle paralysis,' Rutger intoned. 'When the diaphragm muscles freeze, breathing becomes impossible and death soon follows.'

He rubbed the head of the octopus until its lethal tentacles unfurled. 'The blue-ringed octopus may be small, but it carries enough venom to kill twenty-six people within minutes.'

With lip-smacking satisfaction, he added: 'There is no antidote.'

He scooped up a snail with a net and set it on the pool's edge. 'This beautiful marble cone snail is a silent killer. One drop of its venom can fell twenty grown men. Symptoms of a sting can start immediately or appear days later. Victims experience intense pain, blurred vision, swelling, paralysis and death through oxygen depletion. There is no cure. No anti-venom.'

He cast a sly glance at Calvin Redfern. 'Standing by in case we need extra assistance are a stone fish, an electric eel and a sea snake. All of which kill in exotic ways. And, of course, we have the sharks. Scared?'

'No,' came the answer. 'But you should be. When I get out of here, you're going to jail for the rest of your natural life.'

A door opened at the far end of the room and a woman with a face the colour and hardness of a statue stalked in. 'I'm sorry to interrupt, Mr LeFever, but . . .'

'Not now, Francine,' barked Sebastian. 'Can't you see we're busy?'

'Go ahead, Francine,' said Calvin Redfern. 'We have all the time in the world.'

Francine glared at him. 'Mr LeFever, please, we have a problem. Two actually.'

'Two problems? What two problems?'

'There's a man – some sort of volcano expert. He says –'

Laura's heart skipped in her chest. Rupert!

'Use your wits, Francine,' Sebastian said impatiently. 'Get rid of him. Now go back to reception and don't bother us again.'

'Mr LeFever, I'm sorry, but he says it's a matter of life and death. He says we must evacuate immediately because the volcano is about to blow. His Early Warning system has gone into the red. He seemed especially agitated about the two children. He's convinced we have them. What is odd is that this horrible boy . . .'

'Damn and blast the volcanologist's Early Warning system,' shouted Sebastian LeFever. 'We checked the volcano monitor this morning and there was nothing to worry about at all. Nothing. Tell him we have our own experts on the case, and we are sick and tired of him bothering us. If he refuses to go, have security arrest him for trespassing. Rutger, when we're done here, have a word with the Tech department and tell them dancing skeletons, which were put there to frighten people like him away, have had little effect. As I predicted.'

'Yes, sir, Mr LeFever, but it does seem to be smoking and I think I saw some sparks.'

'Francine, I'm not going to tell you again.'

'Yes, Mr LeFever. Uh, one other thing. There's this boy. An untidy, obnoxious sort of a boy.'

Tariq and Laura exchanged glances.

'With the most awful parents.'

'Francine, are you going to give me a biography of every visitor?'

'No, Mr LeFever, but you see the boy has gone missing.'

Laura had to bite her tongue to stop herself from cheering. 'Jimmy,' she told him silently, 'we need you to be as good as Matt Walker today.'

'MISSING!' shouted Sebastian. 'What do you mean, he's gone missing?'

Francine shrank back. 'It's not my fault. He threw a tantrum over the cancellation of the aquarium tour. Don't worry, the doors were secure so he's not in the private part of the building. He's probably hiding in the grounds. His parents are threatening to sue . . .'

'Mr Pike, go with Francine and help this family find their boy,' ordered Sebastian. 'If they give you any trouble, kindly escort them to the shark section. Be sure to show them all the nature they desire and a little more. Am I making myself clear?'

'As crystal,' thundered Large. 'Francine, lead the way.'

Sebastian heaved a weary breath. 'Is it just me or is the game not as much fun as I thought it would be?'

'It'll be fun once the action starts,' Janet reassured him. She reached for the chair lever. Calvin Redfern stiffened.

'No!' cried Laura.

Then, almost in slow motion, two things happened. Tariq bent down as if to tie his shoelaces and rugby-tackled the back of Little's knees. The bodyguard grabbed Rutger's jumper to save himself and both men narrowly avoided falling into the pool. They started yelling at each other and pushing and shoving.

There was a splash. Droplets of cold water splattered Laura and clouded her vision. When it cleared Tariq was in the pool and two snails were creeping towards him.

25

'TARIQ, STAND TOTALLY still; nobody else move a muscle,' Calvin Redfern said in a voice of such authority that even the pufferfish seemed momentarily to obey. 'Rain, untie me so I can help the boy.'

'Not on your life. I know your tricks.'

The octopus unfurled a couple of blue-spotted tentacles. To Laura, standing paralyzed with horror beside Little, the creature was sizing Tariq up for the kill.

'I have a better suggestion,' said Sebastian. 'We'll lower you into the water and you can help the boy from there. You could stand between him and the octopus, for example. That would be entertaining. We weren't born yesterday, so whatever cunning plan you're devising, forget it. You're going in with your hands and feet securely tied.'

Laura wanted to leap into the water and save them both, but the thin bodyguard had her in an unbreakable grip. Besides, it was too risky. Any sudden movement could startle one of the venomous creatures and be the death of her loved ones.

Janet Rain pressed a button on the wall. The red chair tipped Calvin Redfern unceremoniously into the water. His ankles were not entirely healed and he staggered and almost collapsed against Tariq before finding his feet and righting himself. Laura bit back a scream. The octopus was swishing its tentacles like an angry cat.

'Tariq, I want you to use my bound hands as a stirrup and get out of the pool.'

'No,' Tariq said stubbornly. 'I'm staying here with you. My hands are free. I can protect you. Let them sting or poison me instead.'

'Aww, how sweet,' snarled Rutger.

Despite their predicament, Calvin Redfern smiled. 'I appreciate that, Tariq, really I do. You've no idea how much. But didn't you once say you'd do anything for me.'

Tariq shifted nervously. One snail was barely a matchbox length from his left foot. He nodded. 'Yes, I did. And I will.'

'Well, I'm asking you now to get out of the pool,' Calvin Redfern said gently.

Tariq gave him a long look and Laura thought she saw him blink back a tear, but he obeyed without a word. Seconds later he was on the pool edge. Rutger leapt forward with a growl and put him in an arm lock.

Laura thought: Where is Jimmy Gannet? What's taking him so long? Has he been captured himself? Has he called the police?

Just the fact that he was here in the first place gave her cause for hope. If he'd been a good enough detective to use her clue to get himself and his mum and dad to Marine Concern, then maybe he had what it took to get them out of this nightmarish situation. But whatever he was going to do, he had to do it fast.

Janet Rain murmured something into radio. The aquarium door slid open. In came an insect in human form. Laura recognised him immediately from Jimmy's description as the man who'd watched her and Tariq board the *Ocean Empress*. He didn't seem to be made of blood, tissue and bone, but of wire, cockroach limbs and white grubs. He moved jerkily, like a beetle. As he passed, she caught a whiff of chocolate peanuts. He put a feeler in his pocket, scooped out the sweets and tossed them into his bloodless mouth.

Sebastian gave a cold smile. 'Meet the Straight A's most infamous member, our expert on interrogation techniques – what you may think of as torture. We prefer to call him Mr McGee. Mr McGee's here to make sure we do this right. We know you're a slippery customer, former Chief Inspector, and we'd like to ensure that things don't get messy. The floor is yours, Mr McGee.'

Mr McGee swallowed one more mouthful of peanuts and sidled to the poolside. He put on a pair of black rubber gloves.

'What would Matt Walker do?' Laura thought despairingly. 'He'd know what to do in this situation and I don't. I'm clueless.' She did a mental run-through of all the Matt Walker books that involved kidnap, hoping for inspiration. Then she remembered the tip she'd given Jimmy – about how Matt had observed that kidnappers were fanatical about detail. It was the mundane – the ordinary – that they tended to overlook.

Mr McGee picked up the net and surveyed Calvin Redfern like a black widow eyeing its prey.

'I don't believe it!' came a muffled voice, followed by a violent pounding on the window.

Kidnappers and captives turned as one to see the most extraordinary sight. The fleshy face of Bob and windblown, worried countenance of Rita were pressed against the glass. Behind them the sky was black with menace.

'Laura Marlin!' shouted Bob. 'Laura Marlin, is that really you? It's the Gannets from the *Ocean Empress*. Remember us? I say, have you seen Jimmy?'

~ 26 ~

SEBASTIAN COVERED HIS eyes with his hand. 'Why can nothing ever go right?'

He turned on Rutger and Janet with a snarl. 'Didn't I warn you that it would be a disaster bringing these brats along? If there's one golden rule I learned in Hollywood, it's never to work with children or animals. And here we have both.'

'Hi, Bob and Rita! How lovely to see you. Why don't you come into the aquarium and visit us?' yelled Laura before anyone could move to stop her. Little almost crushed her hand.

'One more word and you will join your uncle in the

pool, Laura Marlin,' Sebastian said through gritted teeth. To keep up appearances, he waved and smiled at the Gannets, still framed in the window. 'I do believe you're an unlucky charm. From the very beginning, you have confounded our plans at every turn. Well, no more.'

He turned to the insect man. 'Mr McGee, as you are aware a situation has arisen which you are uniquely qualified to handle. For reasons unknown, Mr Pike, who should have dealt with it, has gone AWOL. Would you mind letting our new friends, the Gannets, into the aquarium? Kindly locate the son. The sharks, I'm sure, would be happy to get to know them.'

Mr McGee became quite animated. 'A pleasure, a pleasure,' he squeaked, and scuttled out of the door.

All this time Laura had been scanning the pool area for the ordinary, the mundane, the everyday thing that the Straight A's might have overlooked. It was now that she saw it: a common garden snail. It was making its way up the side of a plant pot.

'Wait,' she cried as Rutger moved to take Mr McGee's place. In the pool, Calvin Redfern was grey with tension. Beads of sweat dotted his forehead. The octopus had retreated but the snails were converging on him as if he was a particularly attractive rock. 'If you're going to kill my uncle,' Laura said, 'I'd like to at least give him a goodbye hug.'

'Don't push your luck,' growled Sebastian, but he nodded to Little to release her.

Laura stepped away from him, massaging her wrist. She approached the poolside with her head down, as if she were defeated and on the verge of tears.

'Hurry up,' snapped Janet.

As she neared the plant pot, Laura pretended to stumble. In one movement she snatched up the snail, swung and held it close to Celia's cheek. She covered the shell that would have identified it as harmless with her palm but let its coffee-coloured underbelly be seen. The woman let out a scream that could have been heard in Antigua.

Laura wiggled the snail slightly. 'Didn't you mention that a sting from this little creature holds enough venom to kill twenty men?'

The gangster went as white as his suit. Celia let out another piercing screech.

'Please,' Sebastian whined. 'Please. Anything but the snail.'

Rutger's hand crept to his pocket.

'One more millimeter, Rutger, and the snail's going to be snacking on Celia,' said Laura a lot more calmly than she felt.

'LISTEN TO THE GIRL,' Celia cried hysterically. 'SHE IS NOT TO BE TOUCHED. DO YOU HEAR ME? SHE IS NOT TO BE TOUCHED.'

Sebastian wheedled: 'Now Miss Marlin, be reasonable. I can see why you're upset, but I'm sure we can talk it over. There's been a misunderstanding. If you put down the snail we can work something out. You'll have my personal guarantee that you can continue your holiday unharmed.'

'Why don't you get in the pool and explain to the octopus as it wraps its poison tentacles around you that it misunderstood? That you were only joking.'

She moved the snail fractionally closer to Celia's eye.

She felt giddy with fear, but her uncle's presence and Tariq's quiet strength gave her courage. 'Sebastian, I want you to help my uncle out of the pool and untie his bonds. One false move and Celia gets the snail treatment.'

Sebastian rushed to do her bidding. Within a minute Calvin Redfern was out of the pool, his hands free. He flexed his fingers to get the blood flowing again.

Janet, Rutger and Little were in various stages of apoplexy, but they dared not say or do anything that would get their boss's wife killed.

'Fair's fair, Miss Marlin,' Sebastian said. 'I've done what you asked. Let Celia go. If you don't, we are going to make you pay a very high price.'

'I wouldn't count on it,' said Calvin Redfern. He lifted up his hand and Laura was shocked to see a real marble cone snail between his fingers. Crossing the room in a couple of strides, he held the snail to Sebastian's neck. 'The only people likely to be paying a high price are you and your sorry crew.'

He smiled. 'Laura, Tariq, I'm prouder of you than you can possibly imagine, but right now I need you to go for help. Take Celia with you as a hostage in case anyone tries anything.'

'Can't you come with us?' Laura burst out.

He shook his head. 'I'm going to get Janet to tie up Rutger, then she, Sebastian and that scrawny excuse for a bodyguard are going to lead me to the shark tank and we're going to do our best to rescue the Gannets and their boy if he can be found. What was his name?'

From the aquarium came the sound of some unfolding

disaster – a strangled yell, the chime of breaking glass and a waterfall roar.

Tariq grinned. 'Jimmy,' he said. 'His name is Jimmy.'

Out in the corridor, it was immediately apparent that all was not well at Marine Concern. The passage was flooded with water and three turtles were gliding towards them. Laura had been worried that they'd be pounced on by Marine Concern's army of security guards, but the building was eerily deserted. She smiled to herself. Something told her that the flood at least was Jimmy's work.

They passed a room with banks of computer screens. One was showing the news. A shaky camera was focused on the Soufriere Hills Volcano. Smoke and sparks were spewing from it.

'Volcano terror. Montserrat residents urged to evacuate,' read the headline.

'Great,' said Laura. 'We'll escape the Straight A's only to be boiled alive by the volcano.'

'And here I was thinking that this was going to be a relaxing holiday,' Tariq responded.

'Will you stop acting like children!' cried Celia. 'My life is at stake and you're behaving as if you're on a school field trip. You do realise that you're not going to get away with this and that, when my husband and the gang catch up with you, your lives will not be worth living.'

'Where is the nearest phone?' Tariq asked, ignoring her.

'Why should I help you?'

'Well,' said Laura, 'these are your options. Help us and save yourself from being stung by the snail or incinerated by the volcano or both, or...No, that's it. Those are your choices.'

Celia sucked in her cheeks, as if she'd taken a swallow of sour milk. 'Janet's office. There's a phone in there.'

But the phone in Janet's office wasn't working, probably because the water in there was already ankle deep.

'Now you're stuck,' Celia said. 'Any minute now, my husband will come rushing in and then you'll be in trouble.'

The children paid no attention to her. Tariq was at the computer. In no time at all he had contact details for the Montserrat police station and had sent them an urgent email. He scanned the laptop hard drive. There were thousands of files. Most seemed to be in a foreign language or in code. It was impossible to know which were most important. It was while he was downloading some of the bigger ones to a file sharing site that Celia let out another screech, this time of rage.

'You wicked monkeys! You tricked me. My husband will get you for this.'

Too late Laura realised that Celia had caught sight of her reflection in the mirror and seen that the snail was a common garden one, not the deadly marble cone snail at all. Before she could react, Mrs LeFever had caught her a glancing blow across the shoulder, knocking her to the floor. Tariq helped her up as Celia flew out of the room, shouting threats.

He locked the door. 'Let her go. I've found something on the computer that you have to see. It's the original blueprints for this place, showing the old lava tunnel. If we could make it there, we'll get out.'

The door handle jiggled. 'Who's in there?' demanded a male voice they didn't recognise. 'Rutger, is that you?'

Laura ran to the window, but it was made from unbreakable reinforced glass and securely locked.

There were shouts in the corridor. "If I get my hands on those kids,' Janet was saying, 'I'll roast them alive.'

Laura's heart clenched in her chest. Where were Calvin Redfern and the Gannets? Something must have gone badly wrong.

Janet pounded on the door. 'Laura and Tariq, we know you're in there. In case you're wondering where your beloved uncle is, we have him held hostage. If you don't come out, we'll put him back in the pool and this time there'll be no mistakes.'

Laura's hands began to shake. Tariq had climbed onto the desk and was testing the ceiling panels with a steel rod. He looked down at her. 'Don't believe her,' he whispered. 'It's a trap.'

Laura steeled herself to focus. If Matt Walker was here, he'd tell her that there was no place for emotion at a time like this.

Something slammed into the door, making a noise like a bomb going off. Laura almost had a heart attack. Tariq was pulling the chair onto the table. He held out his hand. The door was struck again. So violent was the impact that it seemed to sag on its hinges. Laura climbed onto the chair, and hauled herself into the ventilation shaft because that's what Tariq was asking her to do and she trusted him with her life.

She wanted to unlock the door and promise Janet Rain anything she asked for, so long as her uncle and Jimmy, Rita and Bob were unharmed, but it would be lunacy. Negotiating with the Straight A's would be like negotiating with crocodiles. Nothing they said could be trusted.

The door splintered. Tariq was on the chair and pulling himself into the shaft. He kicked the chair away. It wouldn't detain their pursuers for long, but it was something. The ceiling panel clicked into place. Blackness swallowed them. Voices sounded in the room below.

'Tariq, what do we do now?' Laura whispered.

A huge grin came over the Bengali boy's face. He switched on his torch. It was a miniature one that clipped to the side of his wallet. He never went anywhere without it. 'We're getting out of here,' he said.

THE OLD LAVA tunnel was blocked by plywood planks secured by a couple of rusty nails. Behind them was a wide channel that smelled of rotten eggs. The air was so thick and warm it was like breathing in hot cobwebs. It crossed Laura's mind that they might be saving the Straight A's the trouble of killing them by voluntarily entering a tomb.

It was a sobering thought. They looked along the vent. Scraping noises indicated that the gang was already in pursuit. Either they fled into the unknown or they'd be back at the pool, swimming with the octopus.

They ran. Or, they would have run had they had more energy. Unfortunately the tunnel was mostly uphill. They were effectively climbing the Soufriere Hills. Since they'd had nothing to eat or drink since early that morning and since the air in the tunnel was stale and foul, they soon ran out of steam. A stitch bit into Laura's side.

A yellow stripe of light swept across their backs.

'They're coming,' panted Tariq. 'We have to move faster.'

Laura paused to massage the pain in her side. She gritted her teeth and thought of Skye. If something happened to her, who would take care of Skye? She took a deep breath and picked up the pace.

The swinging yellow light grew brighter. Their pursuers were hard on their heels. Laura risked a glance over her shoulder. Janet Rain and Little were gaining ground.

They were about to run again when she grabbed Tariq's arm. 'Stop, I think I felt something.'

There was panic in his eyes. 'Laura, if we hesitate, we're . . . dead.'

'Cool air. I think I felt cool air.'

He didn't argue. He knew as well as she did that a cold breeze could indicate an exit of some kind.

They backtracked a little way, a terrifying prospect with their pursuers pounding towards them. But Tariq's torch found it almost immediately – a crevice between two rocks, worn smooth by the elements. It was incredibly narrow but there was a chance that a child could squeeze through it. Ignoring Laura's protests, he made a stirrup of his hands and lifted her up. 'If I'm not out in one minute, forget about me and run for your life.'

Laura's voice was muffled as she strained to squeeze through the gap. 'Tariq, I'm not leaving you. Not ever.' But even as she said it she knew that Janet and Little must be almost upon him.

She was out in the night, in the sharp sweet air, when she heard Janet's muffled voice say to him: 'It's all over, kid. One move and you're dead.'

'Don't think,' Laura told herself. 'Just act.' She reached down and Tariq's palms touched hers. 'Jump!' she yelled, and pulled with all her strength.

Tariq's feet found a purchase on the tunnel wall and his head and shoulders emerged from the hole. His face changed. They'd grabbed his ankles.

Laura flung herself on the ground and threw her arms around his chest. 'Leave him alone,' she screamed. 'Leave him.'

He kicked frantically at the monsters below, but it was like battling quicksand. Millimetre by millimeter they dragged him down.

'Run, Laura,' Tariq said weakly. 'Save yourself.'

Laura's muscles felt as if they were on fire, but she gripped him even tighter. 'Tariq, will you shut up and fight.'

He kicked out again and there was a curse from below.

'By dose,' moaned Little. 'You've broken by dose.'

His gripped slacked and Tariq shot out of the hole like a champagne cork from a bottle, barefoot. There were outraged shouts from below as his captors realised that all they had of him was his shoes. And more cursing when they discovered that the hole was kid-sized. Not even Little, with his emaciated, marathon-runner frame, could fit through it.

'This is not the end,' Janet Rain screamed through the gap. 'This will never be over until we've got you and your uncle. We'll hunt you to the ends of the earth. Mr A will insist on it.'

'Good luck with that,' Laura shouted down. 'You're in a lava tunnel and the volcano is erupting.'

There were a few more threats, followed by the echo of fleeing footsteps. The message had hit home.

The children embraced under the night sky. Then they pulled apart, looked at each other and said together: 'The volcano!'

They were on the lower slopes of the Soufriere Hills, just beyond the perimeter fence of Marine Concern. Two reservoirs of water winked in the moonlight.

'Laura,' Tariq breathed. 'Look up.'

A fountain of orange sparks spewed from the top of the volcano. Billowing clouds of red smoke followed, along with molten snakes of black steam and rock. They streamed down the mountain with a tremendous hissing.

'A glowing cloud,' Laura said in awe. 'Heading our way at 700kmph.'

She was spent. She had nothing left to give. Even if it were possible to outrun the volcano, which it wasn't, her body simply was not up to the task.

They started to run, but Laura pulled up with a savage stitch after only a few paces. 'I can't run any more. Not another step. Tariq, you go. Go while you—'

'First, I'd never in a million years abandon you,' said Tariq, raising his voice above the hissing monster. 'Second, there's nowhere to run to.'

There was a ripple of white and then a black shape came hurtling out of the darkness. 'Skye!' Laura could have sobbed with relief. 'Oh, Skye, I've been so worried about you.'

But though the husky was clearly overjoyed to see her, he was not his loving self. After giving her face a couple of quick licks, he began tugging at the bottoms of her jeans with his teeth.

'He's saved us twice before,' Tariq said. 'Maybe he knows something we don't.'

They could see every detail of the swirling red smoke and the lemony glow beneath as a forcefield of gas and rocks sped roaring towards them. It was Laura's nightmare come to terrifying reality.

Faced with the prospect of being incinerated, Laura found to her surprise that she was not nearly as afraid as she'd thought she might be. The conviction that, against all odds, she and Tariq would escape or be rescued blazed as brightly inside her as the molten core of the volcano itself. They had too much to live for. Too many things to do.

Skye barked and worried at her jeans once again. Laura grabbed Tariq's hand. 'The reservoir. He wants us to run to the reservoir.'

They flew towards the nearest tank with the volcano steaming after them. The water was as black as oil. There was no telling how deep it was, or what lurked beneath it.

Laura hesitated. 'What if it's full of sharks? Or worse, snails or jellyfish?'

The glowing cloud was so near they could smell its fiery

breath. 'We'll have to take our chances,' yelled Tariq. 'Just jump.'

They held their breath and jumped.

- 28 -

NEVER IN HER life had Laura seen so many shades of blue. There was soft greeny-blues and pale smoky blues, French blues, Prussian blues, blues like old worn denim, cornflower blues and blues that made your heart feel peaceful.

In the midst of them all was a strip of sparkling white beach. While walking along it earlier that morning, Laura had found a pink conch shell. She'd put it on her bedside table in the room of the private Antiguan villa they'd been loaned for the week. When they returned to Cornwall, she planned to take it with her as a present for Mrs Crabtree, whose wise words had followed her throughout this adventure: 'There's a reason people often put "trouble" and "paradise" in the same sentence, you know. The two words tend to go together.'

The villa came with its own yacht. Her uncle loved to sail and after breakfast that morning he'd taken her and Tariq out into the bay. They'd been drifting on the current, watching rainbow shoals of fish dart in and out of pink and purple blossoms of coral, when a pod of dolphins showed up. Laura would never in her life forget the experience of watching the dolphins play. Their graceful, muscular bodies leapt, somersaulted, and streaked beneath the boat. The spirit of them, their sheer joy at being alive, infused the air around them. It was impossible not to smile in their presence.

One brave dolphin came so near to the yacht they could have reached down and touched it. It chirruped, squeaked and grinned cheekily at them. Then, with a tremendous thwack of its tail, it darted away, leaving them drenched and laughing.

'You look blissed out,' Tariq teased Laura as they sailed back to shore.

'I am,' Laura murmured dreamily. 'In total heaven.'

He grinned. He was blissed out too, just not for the same reasons. Oh, the private villa, delicious food and heavenly stretch of beach were wonderful, especially for a boy who'd known the terror and hardship that Tariq had before meeting Laura. But his past had also taught him that there are more important things in life than beautiful surroundings. Friendship, loyalty and kindness were what counted. That he had found those qualities not merely in his best friend, but in her uncle as well, made his heart feel full to bursting.

He would have laid down his life for Laura knowing that she would, in a second, do the same for him. In St Ives and on Montserrat, she'd proved it.

Back at the villa, Laura threw a Frisbee for Skye before settling into a shady hammock on the verandah. The husky lay on the white boards beside her, washing his sandy paws and licking at his damp belly. He hated to be dirty. He cleaned himself until his wolf-dark fur was once more pristine.

'Be careful what you wish for,' Matron had said time and time again to Laura at Sylvan Meadows. But though Laura would never again buy a raffle ticket, she had no regrets. Everything had worked out for the best.

Not, of course, that it had seemed that way when she'd been sitting at the bottom of a dark tank of water with her lungs burning. At that moment, things had been as bad as they could be.

When she heard Skye barking, she'd propelled herself to the surface, followed closely by Tariq. The husky had heaved himself out and they both used him as a crutch to do the same. Then the three of them had lain still for a long time, gasping for oxygen and coughing in the sulphuric air. Tariq and Laura had used their T-shirts as masks to protect themselves from the toxins, and the boy had tied his handkerchief around Skye's muzzle to protect the dog's lungs. The mountain still streamed with scarlet ribbons, but the area around them was clear.

What happened next was like a sequence from a dream.

Headlights came swerving out of the darkness. The Land Rover and attached caravan bounced into view.

Rupert threw open the door. 'We really must stop meeting like this,' he said. 'Can I offer you a ride?'

When the smoke finally cleared the following morning, Marine Concern had been buried beneath a carpet of grey ash. Thanks to Rupert's Early Warning system and Tariq's email, the Gannets had been saved from the volcano and almost all the gangsters, including Little and Large and the men who'd posed as pirates, were in custody. Almost all. Janet Rain was missing, presumed dead, and Rutger had escaped. Mr Pike was going to jail as soon as he was released from the hospital. He was missing a couple of fingers after losing a battle with a shark.

'Couldn't have happened to a nicer man,' remarked Laura.

Her uncle had had plenty of adventures of his own. He'd been kidnapped from the *Ocean Empress* in exactly the way that Laura guessed – in the conjurer's box. The pirates had taken him directly to Marine Concern, where he'd been held in a dank dungeon dripping seawater until shortly before the children saw him tied to a chair above the pool.

During his stay in the dungeon, Calvin Redfern had expected to be tortured. He'd imagined that the gang would want to take immediate revenge on him for his past success in disrupting the operations of the Straight A's and arresting numerous high-ranking members of the gang.

'Instead, they tormented me by telling me that the two of you had been kidnapped and were being held in Antigua. They didn't let on that you'd escaped. They contented themselves with driving me out of my mind by hinting at how Celia and Sebastian were making you suffer. They promised that my day of suffering would come, but claimed they were waiting for someone. I was certain that that someone would be Mr A.'

Laura put down her drink. 'Mr A?'

She turned to Tariq. 'In over a decade of pursuing the Straight A's, no law enforcement agency anywhere in the world has come close to discovering the identity of the elusive head of the gang.'

'Until last night,' Calvin Redfern put in.

Tariq leaned forward. 'What do you mean?'

Calvin Redfern held his forefinger and thumb an inch apart. 'I was this close to getting him. This close.'

Laura said eagerly: 'Did you see his face? Could you recognise him again? Who was he?'

Her uncle gave a dry laugh. 'I wish I knew. He wore a Joker mask, a hideous thing. His suit was handmade, but there are a million tailors who could have designed it. Mr A has made it his mission in life to eliminate me, so it didn't take a rocket scientist to guess that he was going to be the "guest of honour" at the Straight A's revenge party.

'After you and Tariq had left, I herded Janet and that bodyguard I call Mr Bones into a storage cupboard in the pool area. Rutger was still tied up. There was no lock on the cupboard door but I wedged it shut. However, I knew it wouldn't hold long and I had to work fast. I also knew that it was a matter a minutes before Sebastian realised that he was being held hostage by a dead snail. You see, while I was in the water I'd realised the one of the marble cone snails wasn't moving. When Laura had the genius idea to pretend a garden snail was a killer, it occurred to me that I could do the same with a dead one.'

'What happened next?' prompted Laura.

'It was very obvious that some crisis was unfolding in the aquarium. Water was pouring everywhere and seahorses and a couple of turtles went by. Sebastian was beside himself with fury. At first, we saw no one. My guess was that anyone with sense had escaped the volcano. The same thing must have struck Sebastian because he suddenly made a break for it. As he glanced around, he spotted that the snail was not moving. I could have overpowered him, but I was very worried about your friends, the Gannets, in the hands of Mr McGee.'

He laughed. 'As you now know, I needn't have been.'

Laura and Tariq had already heard the story three or four times, but they made him tell it again. How when he burst into the shark area he'd been greeted by the most extraordinary sight. The adult Gannets were tied up near the dolphin pool. Rita was hysterical. Mr McGee was in the shark tank, being circled by a hungry Great White.

'He was pleading for his life. He looked like a drowning cockroach.'

'And where was Jimmy?' asked Tariq, eyes shining.

'Jimmy was at the instrument panel. As you already know, he'd shown tremendous presence of mind – and courage, mind you – getting past Francine and the guards to make it into the private section of Marine Concern in the first place. Nobody could have blamed him for giving up when he found out the aquarium tour was cancelled, especially since he had no way of knowing whether you and Laura were there at all. And yet he didn't. He was so determined not to let you both down that he threw himself head first down a laundry chute.'

Laura giggled. 'It's such a funny image, although I know it must have been terrifying. When we spoke on the phone, he told me that, as he burst out of the tube, two laundry attendants were standing right there. Luckily they had their backs to him. They were watching television and trying to decide whether or not to flee the volcano. He buried himself under the towels, waited five minutes and found himself alone.'

'Exactly,' said her uncle. 'Of course, then he was in a real quandary. He had to choose between getting away from the volcano himself, or taking a chance that he still had time to rescue you. He chose the latter, which is the reason he's going to be given a medal for bravery.'

'He was doubly heroic,' added Laura, 'because he then opened the door of the aquarium and was confronted with the sight of his mum and dad, whom he thought were still safely in the museum, as hostages. They were roped and bound and that evil Mr McGee was steering them towards the shark tank.'

'The most amazing part of the whole thing is that, by

the time I arrived on the scene, less then ten minutes later, Jimmy was in charge,' said Calvin Redfern incredulously. 'Mr McGee was, as I was saying, floundering in the shark tank, and Jimmy was at the control panel trying to figure out how to save him. If the positions had been reversed that wouldn't have happened, let me assure you.

'At any rate, he kept pressing buttons in the hope of either draining the shark tank or releasing the sharks. Unfortunately, the panel wasn't labelled so the place was awash with water and marine creatures. Each button opened a tank and released a different species. There were turtles and leafy sea dragons everywhere. I was in the midst of untying his parents when two things happened simultaneously. Jimmy hit the button that released both the dolphins and sharks into the sea, and the police ran in. Mr McGee was last seen being washed into the ocean with almost the entire contents of the Marine Concern aquarium, including the creatures with big sharp teeth.'

As soon as he knew the Gannets were safe and would be rescued, Calvin Redfern had dispatched a five-man police squad to find and help Laura and Tariq. That done, he'd raced down to the jetty, where he'd hidden and waited for the gang's notorious leader, Mr A, to arrive.

'I thought there was a good chance he'd be coming by water. What astounded me is that he came alone. Unprotected. He pulled into shore on a sleek little speedboat, already wearing his Joker's mask. He turned off the engine and was preparing to moor when I swam up behind him and put my hand on the edge of the boat. I was so close to him I could have tied his shoelaces. And that's when it happened.'

'What happened?' Laura urged, although she already knew the answer.

He looked at her. 'The volcano erupted. Up on the cliff road, I could see a stream of flashing lights as the police cars and ambulances carried every last person left at Marine Concern out of the path of the glowing cloud. I was sure you were with them. All of a sudden the waves were almost hurricane force. They came in a tsunami-like surge. Somehow Mr A managed to stay aboard and start the engine. He was gone in the time it took me to fight my way out from under the jetty.

'I had seconds to jump into a small motorboat and ride for my life. It saved me from the volcano, but overturned shortly afterwards. Fortunately, the waves had calmed by then. However, I can't say that swimming through an assortment of rare sharks is up there with the most fun I've ever had in my life.'

He grinned at Laura. 'Next time someone offers you the chance to win a free holiday, would you mind counting me out?'

'Don't worry,' said Laura. 'I'll be counting myself out.'

Lying in the shady hammock with Skye snoring softly by her side, Laura allowed herself a small smile. She and Tariq had been praised to the skies by Montserrat's Governor and by Britain's highest-ranking detective for their role in bringing to justice some of the Straight A's most notorious gang members. Of particular help were the files that Tariq had saved to the file sharing site. They proved the business links between the gang and the black marketeers who traded in endangered marine species, and would allow those trade routes to be shut.

But so secret were these findings that the authorities were working to erase all traces of the involvement of Calvin Redfern, Laura and Tariq. No one would ever know they'd been in Montserrat. Apart, of course, from the Gannets and Rupert, but they more than anyone knew the threat the gang posed and their lips were sealed. Besides, Project V, Rupert's Early Warning system, was now being taken seriously and would receive extra funding.

It was odd knowing that no one at school or anyone else would ever know the truth about their adventures, but Laura was fine with that. She agreed with Matt Walker that fame and detection were incompatible. At the same time, it amused her that the Gannets were going to get all the glory.

At some point she must have drifted off, because next thing she knew Tariq was tickling her awake. She opened her eyes. There was a halo of sunshine around him and she thought for a moment how good looking he was and, more importantly, how good. With his white teeth, shiny black hair and caramel skin, he looked as if he belonged to the island. Belonged to Antigua. But, no, she thought, he belongs in St Ives with Uncle Calvin, Skye and I. We belong together, the four of us.

Tariq tickled her again. 'Come on, lazy bones. Let's watch the news.'

~ 29 ~

THE DESTRUCTION OF Marine Concern and capture of some of world's most wanted men was the lead item on the Globe News Network. A presenter wearing a black toupee introduced the day's headlines with the words: 'Meet the ten-year-old British boy whose quick thinking saved hundreds of rare marine species and led to the arrests of some of the leading members of mafia-style gang, the Straight A's. All this while a volcano was raging.'

A picture behind his head showed freckle-faced Jimmy Gannet receiving a red velvet box containing the keys to the island, a gift from the Governor of Montserrat.

After listing the rest of the day's headlines – wars,

floods, cyclones and stockmarket crashes – the presenter returned to the main story.

'And now for some good news. Ten-year-old Jimmy Gannet of High Wycombe in the United Kingdom is a hero for our times. While on holiday in Montserrat, he single-handedly saved some of the earth's rarest marine species from the clutches of the Straight A gang, criminal masterminds responsible for a wave of billion-dollar operations across the world.

'Join us as we go live to the Caribbean island of Antigua, where Jimmy Gannet and his parents are holding a press conference.'

'Jimmy Gannet saves the planet,' Tariq quipped.

'Shh,' said Calvin Redfern. He gave Skye a bone, handed the children a plate of lunch and sank into the sofa between them. 'I'm fascinated by the legend that is Jimmy G. I don't want to miss a word.'

Jimmy was seated at a long table between his parents, a couple of policemen and a media officer. A thicket of microphones separated them from a packed room of journalists. All three Gannets were dressed from head to toe in white. They looked like a party of angels. Jimmy's plump face was positively cherubic. Only the pizza stain on his shirt showed that, beneath the clean laundry, lurked their incorrigible friend.

'Rita, are you surprised that Jimmy saved the day?' asked the smartly groomed Globe News Network reporter, a woman with a blonde bob, wearing a scarlet suit. 'From what you know of your son, are these heroics out of character?'

Rita beamed. 'Not in the least. We always knew Jimmy was special.' She glanced at her husband. 'Didn't we, doll. We believed in him even after he was barred from that crèche. They didn't understand him, you see. They didn't know how to cope with a boy of his intelligence.'

'Exuberant is what he is,' Bob interrupted. 'Curious. Not half asleep like some of the kids you find today. I remember once when Rita brought him down to the factory. I'm in the box business, you see, Gannet Boxes—'

'Mr Gannet,' said the press officer, 'may I remind you that this is a live interview. Let's stick to the subject. Jimmy, tell us in your own words what happened on that day.'

Jimmy flushed. 'Umm, umm . . . It's difficult to explain.'

Watching him, Laura felt a wave of sympathy. It was hard to tell the truth when you had to leave out three of the people involved in order to protect them.

'Jimmy, as I understand it you entered the shark section of the acquarium to find that Mr McGee, one of the world's most wanted and most dangerous men, had tied up your mum and dad. He was marching them towards the tank, with the intention of throwing them in,' said one of the reporters. 'What happened next?'

'Jimmy was very brave,' Rita said.

'Brave as a lion,' Bob added proudly. 'That Mr McGee never had a chance against our Jimmy.'

A huge grin spread over Jimmy's face. In that minute he felt his whole destiny shift. Never again would he be Jimmy Gannet, the prey of school bullies, the shy, clumsy mouse. He'd faced down sharks and gangsters. He was capable of anything.

'Actually,' Jimmy told the reporter, 'it was sort of an accident. When I saw Mr McGee about to throw my mum and dad to the sharks, I ran to try to stop him. I was very scared because this one shark kept opening its mouth and it had thousands of teeth.'

'I'm not ashamed to admit I was screaming,' Rita put in. 'There was a lot to scream about.'

'Go wan, boy. You say it were sorta an accident?' asked a reporter with dreadlocks.

'Yes,' said Jimmy. 'You see, as I ran up to Mr McGee, I tripped over a harpoon gun that was lying on the ground. The harpoon went straight into Mr McGee's leg. He made this strangled noise and fell into the pool with the sharks.'

'It was no more than he deserved,' Rita interrupted, 'and if it was up to me, I'd have left him there. But Jimmy has a heart of gold. He rushed over to this electrical panel and was pushing every other button, trying to find a way to either empty the tank or let the sharks out or something. Bob and I were tied and could do nothing to help. Then the door burst open and this man who looked like a hero from a romantic novel . . .'

'She was hallucinating by that time,' Bob interjected, suddenly remembering that they weren't supposed to mention the tall, dark stranger who'd untied them and dealt with the police with such authority. 'Apparently that's what happens when you get overwhelmed with terror.'

The Globe woman said: 'Some reports are saying that there were other children at Marine Concern that day – a boy and a girl.'

Watching TV, Laura almost choked on her veggie burger.

'How did that get out?'

'There are always leaks,' her uncle told her. 'Don't worry. Your names won't be mentioned. I've made sure of it.'

Bob and Rita looked at one another. 'No, there was only our Jimmy.'

'What do you say to the people who say you're a hero, Jimmy?' the reporter persisted.

Jimmy said, 'I'm no hero. I just did what anyone would have done. I did meet two real heroes once. They saved my life and afterwards they wouldn't even let me thank them for it. They said it was nothing. One of them, the girl, she's going to be a detective when she grows up. She's going to be as good as that detective in the books, Matt Walker. Better probably. You never know, maybe I could be her sergeant or something.'

He grinned. 'Or she could be mine.'

Laura turned off the television. She had a smile on her face, but she was deeply moved. She'd never have believed it a week ago, but she couldn't wait to have dinner with the Gannets that evening. Jimmy, Rita and Bob were coming over to the villa and they were going to have a vegetarian barbecue on the beach. They all agreed that they'd seen quite enough fish for one week.

Laura was particularly looking forward to seeing Jimmy. She'd found a Matt Walker novel in a local bookshop and she wanted to give it to him to inspire him to carry on dreaming and believing that he could do anything. Not, she thought, that he needed a novel. He'd managed very well on his own.

On the phone, however, as in the press conference, he'd

insisted on giving his friends all the credit. 'I learned a lot from watching you and Tariq on the ship,' he told her. 'Firstly, you stand up for yourselves, even against adults, if you think you're right. When the ship's crew and half the passengers were refusing to believe that your uncle had been kidnapped and calling you stowaways, you stood your ground. It was like watching the lions versus the gladiators. I would have run away crying. But you were firm and you held onto the truth and didn't allow yourselves to be bullied.

'There were a couple of other things too. I saw how calm you both were when you saved me at the climbing wall. Other kids – kids like me – would have been boasting and full of themselves, but you and Tariq just carried on without a fuss as if you rescued people every day.

'What helped me most, though, was when you told me about how criminals worry so much about the details that they forget about the obvious stuff. That's what I was thinking about when I saw the laundry chute. They had all this fancy alarm equipment and steel doors and combination locks, but they'd forgotten about the ordinary everyday thing staring them in the face.

'So, thank you,' Jimmy had added.

'For what?'

'For teaching me, for saving me, for being a friend to me and for making this the most exciting holiday of my life.'

'You're very welcome. Thank *you*, Jimmy.'

'For what?'

'For all the same things,' Laura told him. 'We wouldn't

have survived the most exciting holiday of our lives if it
hadn't been for you. Hey, Jim . . .'

'Yeah?'

'Remember what I told you. If you can face down the
Straight A gang, the bullies at your school will be nothing.'

'That's right,' said Jimmy, and she could hear the smile
in his voice. 'They'll be nothing.'

Out on the verandah, Laura allowed herself to revel once
more in the dazzling array of blues. This time in a week,
they'd be in mid-air, on their way back to St Ives. If the
weather forecast was to be believed, it would be raining
when they got there but Laura didn't mind in the least.

Paradise is all very well, but there's no place like home.

Endangered Marine Species – The Facts

~ SHARKS ~

Jaws has given sharks a fearsome reputation as man-eaters, yet in the past five years no more than four people have died each year from shark attacks. Sharks cause fewer deaths than lightning, dogs or falling coconuts. Compare that to our treatment of sharks. We slaughter 70–100 million a year, mostly for shark's fin soup, one of the world's most expensive delicacies. Boat crews often slice off the fins of living sharks and toss them overboard to die a slow, painful death. Up to 10 million kilos of shark fins are exported every year to Hong Kong, a trade hub, which then sends them onto China, Malaysia, Thailand, Indonesia and Taiwan. In the UK, shark meat is sometimes sold as 'rock salmon' in fish and chip ships.

In July 2010, Hawaii made it illegal to possess, sell or distribute shark fins, but it might be too little, too late. Scientists fear that threatened shark species like the Porbeagle, Dogfish, Oceanic Whitetip and Scalloped Hammerhead will be one step closer to extinction by the time CITES (Commission for the International Trade in Endangered Species) meets again in 2013.

WHAT YOU CAN DO: Don't ever order shark's fin soup at a Chinese restaurant or 'rock salmon' in a fish and chip shop. Ask your family and friends to consider joining you in boycotting shark products.

~ TUNA ~

Atlantic bluefin tuna is among the most critically endangered species on earth. Between 1970 and 2007 the Atlantic bluefin tuna population declined by an estimated 82.4 per cent in the

Western Atlantic alone. The tuna is a slow-growing fish that can take up to twelve years to reach maturity and only spawns every two or three years, making them particularly vulnerable to extinction. Yet when did you last see a sandwich shop that didn't sell tuna sandwiches? The black market in tuna alone is believed to be worth over $7 billion a year. Over 80 per cent of captured bluefin tuna ends up in Japan, where it is mostly eaten raw as sushi. In 2010 a single tuna weighing 512lb was sold for $178,000 at Tokyo's Tsukii fish market.

WHAT YOU CAN DO: Stop eating tuna and consider asking your parents and friends to do the same. Ask your school or local sandwich shop to stop serving tuna fish.

~ DOLPHINS ~

A few years ago a BBC survey showed that swimming with dolphins is the activity most people want to do before they die. Across the world, dolphins are suffering horribly to make this dream come true. In places like Japan and the Solomon Islands, wild dolphins are captured and sent off to marine parks across the world. Many of these dolphins die on the way, and the ones who don't are often kept in swimming pools where chlorinated water burns their eyes and skin. Think about how red your eyes are after you've been in the swimming pool. Now imagine chlorine burning your eyes and blistering your skin twenty-four hours a day, seven days a week for ten or twenty years. That's what some dolphins experience. In the ocean, dolphins swim up to 50km a day and live in big, social groups that spend hours every day hunting. In captivity, they are confined, bored, abused, made to perform ridiculous tricks, and fed dead fish, all so someone can say they swam with a dolphin.

WHAT YOU CAN DO: Refuse to visit any facility that keeps captive dolphins. If your dream is to swim with dolphins, wait until you have the chance of swimming with them in the wild, in situations where the welfare of the dolphins is paramount. Better still, content yourself with observing them from boats on tours that respect the dolphins' space and freedom.

~ MARINE TURTLES ~

Six of the seven species of marine turtle are endangered, and yet illegal trade in meat, leather and eggs from these animals continues. In 2009, enforcement officers seized 849 sea turtles from a Vietnamese farmer who was planning to sell them for their meat and shells.

WHAT YOU CAN DO:If you're travelling and are offered souvenir turtle's eggs, leather or shells, refuse to buy them and contact the authorities. Sponsor a turtle family through the Born Free Foundation: www.bornfree.org

~ SEAHORSES ~

The illegal trade in seahorses for use in traditional Chinese medicine is on the increase. In July 2010, a single seizure in Beijing turned up 100 kilos of freeze-dried seahorses. The legal trade is also a matter of grave concern. An estimated eighty nations trade in 24 million seahorses annually.

WHAT YOU CAN DO: Never buy any seahorse product, legal or illegal.

~ SEADRAGONS ~

Leafy and Weedy seadragons are very rare and highly prized by collectors. If you own an aquarium, boycott any shop that sells them and refuse to buy them.

For more information or advice on how to sponsor marine species or raise money for them, contact the Born Free Foundation or join their Born Free Kids club: www.bornfree.org

~ ACKNOWLEDGEMENTS ~

Heartfelt thanks to my agent Catherine Clarke, my editor, Fiona Kennedy, and all the other lovely people at Orion, especially Lisa Milton, Alexandra Nicholas, Nina Douglas, Kate Christer and Jane Hughes. Thanks also to David Dean for the incredible cover, to Anne Tudor of the Born Free Foundation for suggesting the location, and to Carlisle Bay resort in Antigua.

Look out for more mysteries with
Laura Marlin in August 2012.